BEAUTIFUL
BUT BAD

ALSO BY ROBERT COLBY

The California Crime Book
The Captain Must Die
Caught Short
The Deadly Desire
The Faster She Runs
In a Vanishing Room
Kill Me a Fortune
Kim
Lament for Julie
Make Mine Vengeance
Murder Mistress
The Quaking Widow
Run for the Money
Seajack
Secret of the Second Door
These Lonely, These Dead
The Star Trap
Vanished

BEAUTIFUL BUT BAD

ROBERT COLBY

WILDSIDE PRESS

Published by Wildside Press LLC.
wildsidepress.com | bcmystery.com

CHAPTER ONE

Floyd Wyckoff watched from the window of his compartment as another station receded in darkness. The train gathered speed with the gentle ease of streamlined acceleration. Again there was the soft rhythm of movement, dots of light in the jagged dashes of night terrain, and the muted sounds which filtered with dream-like unreality to the isolation of the compartment—like the distant cry of engine to crossing, and then the thin warning bell at the gates, its volume growing in a splash of headlights, diminishing, gone.

Wyckoff plucked the newspaper from his lap and continued his examination of the financial section. But after a moment he yawned and thrust the paper aside. He pulled back the white French cuff of his shirt and studied his watch.

It was a gold watch; smartly modern. The design of the case was unusual, shaped like a diamond, but the face was without numerals; gold hands pointed to ruby chips. The watch had cost fifteen hundred dollars and was presented to him by the senior executives of Wyckoff, Bonham and DeWitt with an appropriate inscription. The occasion was his tenth anniversary as chairman of the board.

He had come to hate the watch because sometimes, in the haste of the moment, he misread the deceptively uncomplicated dial. Presently, it was 8:37. He observed with some irritation, that the train was going to be about forty minutes late into Miami.

Floyd Cameron Wyckoff was a multimillionaire at fifty-one. W. B. and D., a national brokerage house, was only the favourite of his holdings. There were others. He had the controlling interest in an airline, a shipping company and an auto parts chain. With so much achievement he had long ago forgotten the taste of failure and the exhilaration of success. In terms of personal need, he never thought of money at all. But there was still the pride and joy of power. When he spoke, even lightly, people moved to fulfil his smallest wish. His suggestions became orders, and his commands could rearrange the structure of big business and the lives of thousands.

Even now he was conscious of this power, dormant as a great jungle cat who sleeps in his cave and saves his energy for the prey. And with the knowledge of his power there was a feeling of indestructibility, as if the bulwark of ownership and command were almost a physical assurance of immortality.

Yet, like the lateness of the train, though in a larger, more destructive sense, there were unforeseen elements beyond his control. And toward these, Wyckoff was already moving too fast.

He was a big man, tall and imposing. Unlike most of the lesser brass who surrounded him, he was not one of those balding globs of *fat,* as sexual as a side of beef. His dark brown hair was barely touched by grey, and there was an ageless quality in the strong fibre of his body.

His face was square with tough, craggy skin. His eyes were chilled grey. His wide mouth was bold, his jaw demanding. His features were set in permanent lines of self-interest and arrogance.

He watched from the window until the outskirts of the city faded and once again the flat palm-strewn countryside lost character in the blur of speed and darkness. Then he pulled down the shade.

He lighted a cigarette. For a moment he sat tapping his teeth with a forefinger. He looked again at his watch. Frowning, he glanced toward the closed door of the compartment. "Damn," he said aloud. He got up and paced the few steps possible, pivoted and returned. He produced a bottle of Scotch and a glass, added ice from the abundance provided by the porter and a ten dollar bill, and poured generously from the bottle. He picked up the glass and drank.

There was a knock on the door, a gentle furtive sound.

He put down the glass and quickly pulled his suit coat over his white shirt He opened the door and the girl slipped into the room with a little twist of her body, pushing the door closed in the same movement.

"Very good, very good," said Wyckoff, clapping his hands in a mock gesture of approval. "I haven't been waiting much over a half-hour."

"Oh, now, Floyd. I had to eat, didn't I?" She leaned back against the door.

"Sure, sure. You had to eat. But I still don't see why we can't at least take our meals together. I think this secrecy bit has become exaggerated in your mind, Bonnie. It's a little silly." He picked up the glass and swallowed.

"It's for your protection, darling. There are a lot of jealous little people who would just love to tell your wife."

"And your husband?"

"Yes, and my husband. Not that I care—except that he's just the type to make trouble, the brawling kind of trouble that gets into the paper."

"Anyway," said Wyckoff, "I don't know anyone on this train."

"Have you checked every car? Besides, there are many people you've never met in your life who might recognize you. A man in your position has his picture in the paper, has people pointing him out. See?"

"You don't exactly pass for my wife at that," said Wyckoff, smiling suddenly. "Not by twenty years, even if she had half your looks. But—separato meals, separate rooms, separate cars—we might as well be on separate trains."

"Don't I get a drink too, darling?"

He looked at her for a moment, twirling ice in the glass. His jaw relaxed, the shadow of hunger crept into his eyes. He began to fix her drink.

Bonnie reached behind her and with a groping of her hand, locked the door. Wyckoff finished pouring the drink and held it, not offering it to her, waiting for her to come to him. He really liked the way she made such an intrigue of the whole thing. It added an extra dash of spice to the affair. There was a subtle sense of drama in everything she did. And every act carried with it the overtone of her sensuality.

He had known more beautiful women, lots of them. But they were dummies with wooden faces and wooden responses. They fell in love with all the mirrors in all the rooms of the world. And in the intervals between mirrors they were merely actresses in one degree of skill or another, having no truthful appetite for the bed. Bonnie was that real article, the genuine wanton. She gave to sex a kind of cunning imagination and that rare abandon which searches out and invites the secret perversity of desire.

Wyckoff was a man who had seen it all and done it all and had all of it, often with the giant yawn of a rich man's surfeit. And still he knew that Bonnie was the best, though they had met only six weeks ago.

She kicked off her shoes and went toward him with the unaffected grace of a lusty animal. Her hair fell in long waves to her shoulders. It was styled simply, none of the manufactured beauty-shop busyness of curl, or the short tight bob—the creation of fairies to make men out of girls.

He watched the long taper and swell of her body with anticipation as strong as anger. It was good to feel alive and hunger-driven, for there was so little which he wanted or needed any more.

He was about to reach for her but she plucked the drink from his hand and sat down with a little smile of amusement.

"What the hell," he said. "More games?"

"You know me better, Floyd. Won't you wait for tonight?"

The train had slowed and there was the hollow drum of wheels pounding over a bridge.

"I'm not much good at waiting. I gave it up years ago People wait for me now." He dropped down beside her.

"I know," she said. "And isn't this a refreshing change?"

"Listen, Bonnie, don't give me a hard time. Understand?" But he rather liked her independence. All the others had been so damn docile. "You put me off last night, too."

"Do you think it was fun for me? I told you, I didn't want the porter, the conductor or someone else catching me sneaking in and out of here in the middle of the night. I shouldn't be here now. When I leave, you'll have to check first to see if anyone's around."

"Hell, next time I'll hire a special car."

"It's just another hour or so to Miami," she said.

"We pulled out of Palm Beach forty minutes late. The railroads don't give a damn about time any more, even on these express runs from New York. They want to discourage the passengers so they can haul nothing but freight. Sure you wouldn't rather stay at a hotel?"

"No." She shook her head vigorously. "Remember, Miami used to be my town. I know a lot of people there. I don't want to take a chance running into someone."

"Well, I don't suppose this girl friend of yours and her husband think you want to use their house for charades."

"Jane and Vince are two people I can trust, no questions asked."

"Sure they won't come barging in?"

"Never. They were glad to stay over at the beach for a week-end, especially after I sent them your two hundred bucks. To them, that's a lot of money. Now don't worry—and don't expect the kind of palace you're accustomed to. It's just a little house, two tiny bedrooms and a bath."

"On the contrary," he said. "I'm looking forward to it. You bet I am." He put his arms around her and pulled her close. She settled against him with a sigh.

"Love me?" she said.

He groaned. "Don't start that. Don't play any moonlight songs for me, honey. I told you from the beginning where I stand."

"Wouldn't you rather be married to me?"

"I'd rather be in bed with you than anyone else. I don't want to discuss the rest of it again. Period. If you want an end to this, you're on the right track."

"All right, all right. Sorry. That's the last time. You'll see."

"Good. Good girl." He lifted her chin and kissed her, meaning it to be a sort of handshake. But the kiss got away from him. For a moment she resisted, fingers pressed against his chest. But then she made a sound in her throat and turned her body toward him.

The train leaned around a curve and hurtled them into the night.

CHAPTER TWO

He saw her standing at the curb in front of the Miami station as he drove up. She looked anxious, a little strained, and still exciting, even after the session on the train. He opened the door and she handed him the overnight case. He tossed it in back and she ducked inside, first glancing around to see if anyone had noticed her. While he had claimed the car from the rental agency, she had gone to the drugstore in the depot for, "What the add people call beauty aids, darling."

He released the brake and swung into traffic.

"Turn right at the next corner," she said. "It's quite a way, I'm afraid. But then, it's very private."

He made the turn.

"It's a beautiful car, Floyd."

"Glad you like it," he said without enthusiasm.

"I didn't know you could rent a brand-new Cadillac like this."

"You can rent anything for a price," he said. "Or any *one.*"

He felt her eyes on him and he almost smiled.

"Of course," she snapped. "And I'm cheaper by the week—so why do you take me for just a couple of days?"

"Oh, I can afford it, I think." He chuckled.

"That's not funny, Floyd. If I was interested in your money it would take a lot more than a few presents that I have to hide most of the time anyway. Please make a left at the next corner."

"You're too sensitive, Bonnie. I was joking. If you ever did need money, you'd only have to ask. I know you don't have much, but I never wanted to embarrass you." He braked and tugged the wheel left.

"Money doesn't really embarrass me," she said, "except in small quantities. A hundred dollars would embarrass me, but a thousand would not be quite so embarrassing. Understand?"

"In the morning," he said. "I'll make you out a cheque for five thousand. Then you needn't blush at all."

He was irritated. He had especially liked Bonnie because there was no financial arrangement between them, and the degree of her passion had therefore flattered him. But this kind of talk worried him. It made him aware of his constant need to be self-protective.

"Five thousand," she repeated. "That's very nice—very. But as a matter of curiosity, would you say I'm worth more?"

"Oh, a lot more." Now that she had opened the subject, he was impelled to see what was on her mind.

"How much does your wife spend a year, Floyd?"

"I couldn't tell you that, even if I wanted to. She has a more or less unlimited bank account of her own." He stuck a cigarette in his mouth and pressed the dash lighter.

"A hundred thousand? Two hundred?"

"Perhaps."

"Would I be worth two hundred thousand a year to you?"

"No," he said coldly.

"Why not, if I'm so much better in bed?"

"Because you're not a permanent fixture in my life, for one thing."

"Ahhh," she said. "That's what I really wanted to know. How long could I last, Floyd? A few more weeks or months, a year?"

"I couldn't say, Bonnie. Not long at all if you're going to complicate it like this. I'm extremely busy with important decisions and I can't afford any outside pressures."

He stopped for a traffic light and got the cigarette going without offering her one.

"If I got a divorce, would that make me at least a permanent side line?"

"I can't make any promises, Bonnie. And I think you would be very unwise to get a divorce on such a gamble."

The light changed and he shot ahead. He knew this sort of thing would come up sooner or later. It always did. What she probably wanted was to be on the payroll as a second wife, the kept woman in the penthouse apartment, spending recklessly, with about the same abandon as she made love. Never—and not because he couldn't afford it. But she was not nearly the companion that Margaret was; there could never be that closeness or affection. In fact, in the spaces between those frantic sessions, he was not even sure he liked her very much. No, it wouldn't last. Better that she learned it now. Otherwise, a parting could get messy.

"Don't push me, Bonnie," he said. "I don't push, you know. If you want to make some reasonable arrangement with me financially, that's okay. You'll find me generous enough. But it's temporary. I've never kidded you about that."

There was a silence in which his resentment diminished and his remoteness grew. He wished now that he was going directly to Harvey Burnett's house on the bay instead of killing the weekend in petty bickering, being wheedled by Bonnie for the sake of an urge—the one weakness he could never quite master. Tomorrow he could be fishing in the stream over the transom of Harvey's yacht.

As the silence lengthened between them, they left the city proper and sped through a suburb.

"Darling," she said then. "Don't be angry. I was never serious for a minute about the money. I wouldn't take a cent from you. It would cheapen the whole thing. I just wanted to know where I stood."

"Well, you can still have that cheque in the morning, Bonnie. I meant it."

"I won't even talk about it. And I do admire your honesty, Floyd."

"Let's forget it, then," he said, feeling relieved, his good humour returning in a rush. "Let's just forget it."

"Forgotten," she said breezily. "All forgotten. Now, turn left at the next traffic light."

"I should phone Harvey Burnett. He's expecting me in the morning and I'll have to stall him."

"Darling, you had plenty of time to get in touch with him."

"No, I wanted to make it casual, a last-minute change. I'll tell him I met someone on the train."

"Well, you can call him from the house," she said. "They have a phone."

"Good. Would you like a cigarette?"

"Yes, thank you."

It seemed a long and involved drive, taking better than a half-hour, but Wyckoff enjoyed it. The night was balmy, the tepid air pleasant after the biting chill and snow of February in New York.

"We're almost there now," she said. "About another quarter-mile."

"When will your husband be back from San Francisco?" he asked.

"Next week," she answered. "And I'm *not* looking forward to it. He's a louse and I hope you never meet him, darling."

"Don't worry."

"There," she said in a minute. "Just up ahead on the left. Slow down."

They were driving on a narrow road, lined with very few houses and those widely separated. He lifted his foot from the accelerator.

"That little white house," she said. "Naturally they didn't think to leave a light. Well, just pull into the drive."

He braked and swerved, came to a stop, cut the motor and lights.

He got her suitcase and then his own from the trunk. He carried the bags to the door and she fumbled around beneath a mat.

"Such an obvious place," she said. "I'll bet you could collect a hundred keys in an hour just searching under door mats. Here—I found it!"

After a couple of stabs she got the key in the lock and turned. They entered. She fumbled for a switch, flicked on the lights, closed the door. It was a small living room cluttered with nondescript furniture and throw rugs. The blinds were drawn, the windows closed. It was stuffy and there was an odour peculiar to the inhabitants. In spite of his expectation that it might all be fun, he looked around with distaste. He dropped the bags and sighed.

"Would you like to see the rest of it?"

Floyd smiled faintly and nodded.

They moved into another room and she pressed another switch. She stepped away from him and leaned back against a high bureau.

There were three men in the room—two in chairs and one reclining comfortably on the bed, pillowed up against the headboard. The men wore slacks and sport shirts. Their faces reflected a mixture of curiosity and amusement.

The man on the bed had size over the others. Tanned biceps bulged from the short-sleeved shirt, dark eyes looked out from a sullen face upon which the smile seemed incongruously drawn. A big hand rested lightly around the butt of a .45 automatic on the bed. The hand lifted the gun almost casually.

"Floyd," said Bonnie. "I'd like you to meet my husband."

"A real pleasure, Mr. Wyckoff," said the man on the bed. His grin widened.

"Yes, sir, Mr. Wyckoff. I want to tell you, it's a real pleasure."

CHAPTER THREE

On a Monday morning in New York two days later, Bryan Wyckoff awoke to the sound of music. The music throbbed from beyond his bedroom door. He covered his head with a pillow but the beat was so insistent that a thin hammer of sound still echoed rhythmically in the chamber of his skull. After a minute of tossing, he thrust the pillow aside and sat up, stretching his lithe, young body.

He smoothed the black disorder of hair and then with his palms squeezed his temples in a rotating motion. *A very slight headache, considering,* he thought. *Well, you had to stay reasonably sober when you were hosting your own party.*

Bryan glanced unnecessarily at the empty space beside him on the double bed. That would be Donna playing his hi-fi, hinting that she wanted company. Donna was a young actress who did bits on Broadway and was currently "between plays". She was a hangover from the party. She had arrived alone and then by prearrangement, remained hidden in Bryan's bedroom until the guests had slopped out the door, embarrassing the silence of the hall with their raucous farewells.

Bryan got out of bed and pulled a robe over his shorts.

He went to the window and with his fist, cleared a round space on the frosty pane. A light snow fell indecisively, the little flakes scattered by quick currents of wind. The day settled like a grey shadow above the darker grey of the Hudson River. Twelve stories below the apartment house, buses, taxis, cars, moved in a nodding cadence along Riverside Drive. The pace was faster on the stilted roadbed of the West Side Highway in the background, while the few pedestrians, darting over the walks of the Drive, huddled into their overcoats, leaning against the wind, scurrying for shelter.

Bryan blinked his eyes and squinted at his watch—11:25. He usually got up at noon and stabbed at his typewriter until six. He'd have to get rid of Donna because there was a certain self-discipline he demanded. *All right, get rid of her, but not too fast.* He smiled. He might pay the penalty and work until seven.

Bryan Wyckoff, like his father, was a lot of man. Actually, he was an inch taller, there was more spread to his shoulders and he was deeper in the chest with a leanness of torso that his father had lost. He had the same block of jaw but the nose was less prominent, the cheekbones higher.

It was a dominant face but did not bear his father's look of arrogance and self-interest. At twenty-nine he was as widely separated from his father by attitude as by age. Bryan often said that he and his father had a single meeting ground, and that was the ground upon which you could find all women worth meeting.

He crossed the room now and paused, listening a moment to the strident pulse of a cha-cha before opening the door and peering into the living room.

Donna stood with her back to him. She was sipping from a cup of coffee, tapping her foot from side to side, her tawny hair swaying about her neck. She wore nothing but one of his giant maroon bath towels, knotted at the side. She put down the cup and began a few experimental steps until she was furiously involved in the whole dance with all its breaks and twirls. Her movements carried her in full circle so that she must have seen him, though she pretended oblivion.

Soon the towel worked itself loose and fell to the floor. She gave it a kick and her breasts surging with the tempo, danced toward him.

She came within a few steps of him, said, "Hi!," went undulating past and returned. He grabbed her.

"You've got a lot of talent," he said. "But it's all vertical. What a waste, what a waste!"

Arms around him, she danced in place.

"You'll have to forgive my appearance," she said. "I just came out of your shower."

"I'll never wash that towel, Donna. I'll keep it under my pillow always—for lonely, lonely nights."

"Oh, lonely, lonely one," she breathed, dancing on. "Anyone for coffee? I just burned up a new batch."

"This is no time for coffee!"

He stepped backward into the bedroom, pulling her along until his legs touched the bed. They fell limply together and with a little bounce of the mattress, lay still. Her face had grown serious, intent. Her lips opened and suddenly locked against his. He ran his hand down her smooth, supple body.

The phone rang.

"Hell," he mumbled.

"This is not time for Alex Bell, darling. Ignore him."

He went back to kissing her and might have forgotten the phone altogether, especially since the sound came distantly from the room he had made into a study. But the bell continued to ring relentlessly, intruding upon his consciousness, trampling desire.

"Someone means business," he said. He got up and gave her thigh a pat. "Back in a minute, lover. Don't start without me."

He moved with long easy strides through the living room, noting in passing the grey muck of ash and twisted butts in the swollen trays, the scatter of drink-grimy glasses and half-chewed sandwiches. Someone had dropped a cracker laden with cheese dip upon one of the turquoise cushions of his sofa.

At least one slob in every damn crowd, he thought. *The hell with parties—my own, that is.*

He snatched the receiver from the cradle and sat on a corner of his desk.

"Don't you ever give up?" he said.

"Bryan! I thought you never would answer."

"Hello, Mother. It's been quite awhile. What is it now? You want more money?"

"Now, please, Bryan, be serious and just listen. I need you, dear. Your father—well, he's in trouble."

"Dad? Impregnable, invincible Floyd Wyckoff? Impossible!"

"Bryan, this is not funny and I asked you to please just—"

"What's dear old Pater been doing—cheating on his income tax? I suppose he won two-three hundred thousand from Charlie DeWitt at golf and forgot to mention it. Just like DeWitt to report him." Bryan reached over the desk, opened a drawer and produced cigarettes. "Or is it a dame this time? Well?"

"Bryan—I want you to put aside your personal feelings about your father and I want you to come over here right away." His mother spoke in that cool, soft tone which had made him hop as a boy.

"Is that an order?"

"That's ... that's an order, dear, if you love me." And then suddenly she was crying.

"All right," he said, "All right, Mom. I'm sorry. I didn't realize. Of course, I'll be over. Can't you give me something to kick around on the way? What's it all about?"

"I don't think we'd better discuss it on the phone, Bryan." She came back strong, in control.

He had forgotten the cigarette and now he got it going with the table lighter.

"Can't tell me a thing, eh?"

"Just this—your father has disappeared. He never arrived at Harvey Burnett's in Miami. He was supposed to have been there two days ago. There's a lot more which I'll tell you later. Try to make it in twenty minutes. Now don't fail me, dear."

She began to cry again. Then she hung up.

Donna was in bed with a sheet drawn up under her chin. Her sexy little grin of welcome seemed misplaced and now somehow she was a stranger.

"What's the matter?" she said. "You look terribly sincere."

"I'm afraid our little, game has been called, lover girl Some family rain has fallen. That was Mater and she just ordered a command performance at the domicile on Park in twenty minutes."

"Oh? I thought you *never* went there any more."

"Never when the Old Man is on tap. He's not. Got to shave, dress and take flight, honey. Sorry."

"You want me to leave?"

"Well, it's just going to be a scramble from here on in. I'll be distracted. You might not get more than a grunt out of me."

"I could stay and clean up for you. Then, later—"

"No, I think you'd better crowd into some clothes and I'll give you a call when the storm's over. Thanks anyway, Donna."

"Too bad," she pouted. "I was "hoping that we—"

"Oh, hell!" he exclaimed, annoyed. "Now listen, I don't have time for the usual crappy dialogue of sweet parting. I've got trouble—plenty!"

He strode off to the bathroom. He had forgotten her by the time he had the razor plugged in and whirling.

It didn't sound good, the Old Man missing. His father was not a type to wander off into space, out of contact. Whatever he was, he always kept in touch, at least with the office. Big, big, big decisions rested on his shoulders. Anyway, *he* thought so and, in effect, that was the same thing. No, he'd have to keep a line to the office, and of course his mother had checked there, or she wouldn't be phoning.

His mother could be exaggerating under some emotional strain—like the discovery of a new filly in the Old Man's ever-changing stable—but that was unlikely. His mother had weathered other such situations with disdainful calm and confidence. She might run rivers inside, but on the surface she was dry as a bone. He had never seen her erupt in tears except in a major calamity or sadness, as at the death of his grandfather whom she had loved dearly.

This was special. Floyd Wyckoff must be in deep trouble.

So? Did he care? Hell, that was a lousy way to think about his father—or was it merely honest?

Donna was speaking over the buzz of the shaver. "Well, I'm dressed and on my way," she called from beyond the bathroom door. "Have fun!"

"Kay," he mumbled. "Sorry. Forgive."

She said something else but he didn't get it, wasn't really listening. In a moment he heard the door slam, a sound of hurt and defiance.

Once he had been quite devoted to his father. That was in the naive time before the Old Man sent him off to West Point ("... above all, the sons of rich men should learn discipline."), before he had an inkling of what he wanted to do with his life, before his grandfather's death and the trust fund inheritance.

Floyd Wyckoff Senior, another dynamo of finance and acquisition, had left Bryan the income from a quarter million. He was not to have the principal until he was thirty-five, for his grandfather believed that a man had little understanding of his real direction and the uses of money until a kind of second maturity accrued in the mid-thirties. True enough, Bryan agreed, but the income from a quarter million would sustain a man of modest needs very well. And since Bryan was not driven by the same urge to power and dollar multiplication of his father, the trouble began.

The trust income became his a month before his graduation from the Point, and with it the first feel of independence and a new thoughtfulness. Strongly against his father's wishes, he went on to complete a hitch in the Army Air Corps, perhaps searching for his own direction in the sky, perhaps only seeking the thrill of jet propulsion. But he decided that some sort of career in flying would, like football, pale with repetition, droop for lack of further challenge.

He had been a star fullback and might have accepted the invitation to play pro. He had considered the possibility quite gravely. But having once achieved a top place in some endeavour, he quickly lost interest. What could follow but more of the same? Also, he was too analytical to be content with continuing in a mere game. So you carried a leather ball across a field against opposition, using a strategy which had just as many variations, and eventually you reached a goal post and set the little ball down and the idiots cheered—so what? Could you do that over and over for even part of a lifetime?

No, he was much too analytical. After a time he saw nearly every pursuit as a rather childish game to indulge the vanity of grown men.

He did not re-enlist in the Air Corps, did not want a career in commercial aviation. It was a time of crisis. His father thought that he had burned out his desire for excitement and change, that he would now plant himself firmly in one of the Wyckoff enterprises and prepare to "take the reins." His brother, Van, was already entrenched at Wyckoff, Bonham and DeWitt, being groomed for a vice presidency.

"A man past twenty-one should not vacillate," said Floyd Wyckoff. "He should know what he wants to do, leap in aggressively and make a worthwhile contribution to the world, else the world will soon learn to spin without him."

"Sounds pretty," said Bryan, who unlike Van, was not cowed by his father. "But it's a lotta crap! With all due respect, of course. Only a handful of pseudosaints do anything that could strictly be called a 'worthwhile contribution.' The rest simply please themselves, by whatever name they call it, or they're forced by circumstances into some agonizing pattern of slavery before they ever have time to get well enough acquainted with themselves to understand what the hell it is they'd really like to do. And so-called big business on the executive level is only worth-while if you happen to get a bang out of it. I've had a few summers to poke my nose in, get the smell of power-dealing in finance, shipping, aviation. No thanks. I'm positive it would bore me in three months. I'm grateful for the opportunity because not many of the poor jokers out there have it. But thanks a lot, no thanks."

"All right," said his father, "all right. I'm not unreasonable. I won't pressure you into taking a position with one of the Wyckoff holdings. I'm not one of those cliché fathers who demands a carbon-copy son. But dammit, do something! Get into some other organization and move up. Now! Grow up, stop wasting time!"

"I don't give a hoot about organizations of any kind. An organization is a big, solemn, regimented game—like the Point, like football, like the Air Corps. I don't want to be regimented. And I'm not ready to move in or up, anywhere."

"What *are* you going to do then?" asked his father with disgust.

"I don't know. I might play piano, or tuba. I might paint, or write, or race horses, or fight bulls. Whatever I do, I'm going to enjoy it. I don't need yachts, pink champagne and caviar, mansions or Cadillacs. So I can afford to wait. Meanwhile, I'm going to travel around the world and think about it Period!"

Bryan had been perfectly sincere and he had done exactly what he said he was going to do. That was four years ago and his father had not spoken to him since. There had been no communication between them except for one piece of mail—a photostat of an excerpt from his father's will. The paragraph concluded that after careful consideration, son Bryan had been judged irresponsible, frivolous, incompetent and unworthy to receive and manage his share of the Wyckoff holdings and/or monies. He had been left the sum of one dollar.

Bryan went into the bedroom and opened the closet. He grabbed a suit and tossed it on the bed, went to the bureau for a shirt. His ties were sorted on the rack according to colour and he snatched the first blue one his fingers touched. He pulled on his clothes with mechanical haste.

The day's work would be lost. Ah hell, what did it matter now? Anyway, his first novel was moving well. After some awkward starts and rewrites he had hit the stride, found the rhythm of progress. Maybe he'd have more luck inside the wider boundaries, the lesser restrictions of a book. In three years of crushing effort he had sold only two short stories, both to minor publications in the quality group, and for payments that were ridiculous. His work was rejected elsewhere on the grounds that it was too intellectual, too special for the masses, and again, too analytical.

He was unable to compromise, though he understood the need for escape entertainment There was so much careless acceptance of silly platitudes as guides to "right living," so many moronic dogmas leading to unquestioned conformity, so much hypocritical crud behind the false posing of the self-righteous (like his Old Man) who were "leaders of men." It all needed exposure, and he had found his challenge.

At first, when people asked him what he did for a living, he said he was a writer. The stir of interest lasted not much longer than it took to find out he had not yet been published. Then the faces changed, and likewise, the subject.

He was not wounded. It was a rather expected reaction. It gave weight to a measured cynicism that added style to his writing and his living. There were a chosen few to whom he allowed access to his private self. But now, to all others, when asked his line of business, he solemnly replied, "I worked hard until I was twenty-one. Then I retired."

Bryan was wrestling with the big overcoat, moving to the door. He paused with his hand on the knob. *What the hell,* he thought. *Why do I run like a wound-up robot just because he turned up missing? He wouldn't even spit if I was on fire. What's he got a fair-haired boy like Van for? The hell with him!*

For a long moment he stood looking across the living room to the study and the yellow phone on his desk. Then he shrugged and went out the door.

CHAPTER FOUR

Bryan gave his coat to the butler and stepped into the living room of the Wyckoff penthouse with the slight feeling of oppression which the room always gave him. Perhaps it was because of the high ceilings, the over rich French Provincial furniture with its sombre wood and fabric, the perpetual duskiness of the place—or perhaps it was the effluvium of his father, the taint of a personality which clung to the atmosphere.

Margaret Wyckoff came into the room with quick, little steps and characteristic lift of the head, a faint, sad smile on her face. She was a small, dainty woman with fragile, bone-clear features. Her hazel eyes were wide, deep-set and electric. Her dark hair brushed around her head in a neat feather cut. Except for the tiny folds of skin beneath her eyes and the small oblique gullies which marked the corners of her mouth, she seemed still youthful.

She had a pert bird-like attraction, yet there was a valiant quality to the set of jaw and mouth.

Bryan embraced her and she gave his cheek a little pat before turning to pluck a cigarette from a tray with a darting, nervous movement. He gave her the light and she exhaled on a long sigh.

"Thanks for coming," she said. "I know you were reluctant and I understand why, Bryan. But this is not something I can handle alone."

"I gathered that Mother. But what's happened to our boy, Van, favourite son and heir to the throne? He'll never pick up marbles unless he stays in the game, you know. I mean, why me instead of a member of the old team, Mom?"

"Please, Bryan, any other time. I don't want Van for this."

"Oh! Why?"

She sat down carefully, fingering a pearl necklace.

"It's going to take a special kind of handling and judgment," she said. "It's a very—it's a dangerous situation. Van is loyal and he's good at business. But he lacks your directness and animal courage."

"What you mean," said Bryan, "is that he's a gutless wonder. He's a born stooge and it's going to make him a millionaire."

"I hope you're not jealous of him, Bryan."

"I'm *not,*" he said honestly. "I had the same chance to fanny-kiss my way into good grace. I didn't want to pay the price and I've never regretted it. But I'm not going to pretend that I like my father—or Van, either. It seems to be absolute doctrine in this world that there is an almost inviolable sanctity about Family. The same blood has got to be good because it is the same. Crap! Father, mother, brother, sister—just labels for purposes of identification. In my book, relatives don't get a free ride. They have to earn respect like anyone else."

"Aren't you even curious about what's happened to your father, Bryan?"

"Not particularly." He crossed to a window and looked down upon the winter-bleak islands of Park Avenue, the scuttering traffic, the green-red blink of the lights behind the erratic dance of snow. "No, not particularly. I came because *you're* curious."

"Oh," she moaned, "I'm so much more than curious."

He turned sharply. "Well, I might work up just a grain of sympathy if I understood. Tell me about it—from the beginning."

She smoothed her brow with a trembling hand, took a deep breath.

"Floyd went to Miami to spend a week with Harvey Burnett They had some business matters to discuss, but mainly Floyd wanted to get in some fishing and take a rest. I loathe fishing, I despise Claire Burnett and I wasn't anxious to go. Anyway, Floyd discouraged me from the beginning. He was rather strange ... I won't go into that now.

"As always, he took the train. He never got over just missing that Chicago plane, the one that crashed—you remember. Anyway, he simply won't ride in a plane. Well then, he was due to arrive in Miami sometime Friday night. Because of the lateness of the hour he was going to stay at a hotel, the Fountainbleau, and go on out to Harvey's in the morning. He was going to phone me Sunday, at the latest.

"Sunday night I did get a call, but it was from Harvey. 'Where's

Floyd?' he said. 'We were expecting him yesterday. He didn't call, hasn't shown up and isn't registered at the Fountainbleau—never had a reservation, in fact.'

"Well, I told Harvey I was as mystified as he was. Had he checked any other hotels? Yes, he had checked the leading ones on the beach and in the city. Nothing. He had also phoned other friends of Floyd's in Miami, asking very discreetly because he didn't want to start any crazy rumours. No one had seen him. Harvey did find out that he was on the train, that he got off at Miami and rented a car from one of those car-rental places—also, that he was alone."

She looked at Bryan carefully a moment, then dropped her eyes.

"We decided to wait until noon today," she continued.

"Then Harvey was to get in touch with the Miami police. But at nine-thirty when the mail came, this was in it."

She passed him an envelope which had been resting under a table lighter. He opened it and read from a typewritten sheet.

> We are holding your husband. He has not been harmed. But he will die if the following instructions are not followed exactly:
>
> 1. Do not inform police! Do not inform anyone!
>
> 2. Send one messenger with the ransom (six hundred thousand in used twenties, fifties and hundreds) to Miami train departing New York 10.40 p.m. Tuesday. Contact will be made somewhere between New York and Miami. Contact will present personal item belonging to Wyckoff as identification. Pick up reservation under name Richard C. Brown, Car A-153, Compartment B.
>
> If police on train, Wyckoff will die! Release will follow delivery within twenty-four hours.
>
> There will be no second chance.
>
> Do not fail!

Bryan read the note twice with astonishment.

"Hell," he said. "How could such a thing happen?"

"I don't know," said his mother, "but it has. And now we've got to deal with it."

"Dad once told me that when we were kids he was aware of the danger of kidnapping. He never left us unguarded. But I don't suppose it ever occurred to him that he—have you called the police?"

She shook her head vigorously. "There will be no police until he's released. I've thought about this until I'm nearly out of my

mind! Oh, how I wish I *could* call the police. But I keep remember-
ing those kidnapping stories I've read in the papers. Usually it's
just a little baby that you wouldn't think anyone but a fiend would
harm. And yet, ninety percent of the time, as soon as the police are
called, the baby is murdered—" Her voice broke.

He crossed the room and laid his hand gently on her head.

"Yes," he said. "It's true. And then sometimes the money is
paid and the victim is killed just the same." He lifted her chin. "I
don't want to scare you, but you've got to see both sides."

"I know, I know!" Her voice rose hysterically. "But once you
stir up the police, somehow it always leaks to the newspapers, no
matter what the police promise. And then there are the headlines
screaming at the criminals, making them feel the whole country is
looking for them, every citizen a threat, and they get scared. And
when they get scared, they—they kill and run."

Nodding, Bryan sat down. "You're right. There has to be another way." He studied the note, reading the lines, trying to read
between them.

"Van is raising the money," his mother said. "I can't get my
hands on that much cash. Van is selling some securities which
Floyd put in my name."

"When will the money be ready?"

"I'm not sure," she said. "Van will know. I'm expecting him
any minute ... Bryan?"

"Yes?"

"Will you do it? Will you take the money to that contact on the
train?"

"Was there ever a doubt in your mind?"

"Yes—because of your attitude toward your father."

He smiled wryly. "Don't worry. Unless I can keep him alive,
how can I go on playing the maverick?"

"Then you don't hate him?"

"Hatred is the luxury of people who have time to sit around
enjoying it. Truthfully, I haven't thought of him at all for quite
awhile now." He lighted a cigarette and glanced again at the note.
"It says here that contact will be made somewhere between New
York and Miami. That's pretty vague. It's a long trip. There's got
to be a purpose behind that word 'somewhere.' Certainly the sort
of hoods who can engineer the kidnapping of a man like Floyd

Wyckoff aren't so dumb that they don't see the danger to their contact. It's a pretty damn nervy arrangement—over-confident, risky. I don't figure this at all. Strange ..."

"Such a nightmare," she said. "I can't believe this loathesome thing has happened to us. Oh, I can hardly breathe! You will be careful, dear? Who knows what they have in mind? There could be an element of danger for you, too."

He smiled. "Is that why you didn't want to send Van?"

"Now, you know better than that, Bryan." Her eyes were soft and moist. "You can't pretend that I don't love you more than anyone in this world but your father."

"Sure. I just wanted to needle it out of you."

"But—I thought Van might get jumpy under pressure and bungle the whole thing," she continued.

"Yes, well just count on cool, cool Bryan. I've had so much experience at this sort of intrigue, you know."

It seemed to Bryan they were talking about someone else, not his father. The thought came swift as a sneaky blow to the gut. He *could die. The Old Man might already be dead. Mustn't let it show in my face—casual now, sound breezy and confident—or she'll come apart.*

He studied the envelope in which the note came. "Mailed from Miami," he said. "Well, at least we know he's probably somewhere in that area. Big help that is."

A door closed and Van Wyckoff came in the room, moving with nervous haste, the butler trailing behind him as he shed his coat. He was a year older than Bryan, not as tall and slightly plump in a pallid, flabby sort of way. He had a round face, fleshy at the cheeks. His mouth was small with a turned-back, girlishly petulant underlip. He wore black horn-rimmed glasses which seemed too large for his face and behind these, his small, dark eyes were charged with a fatuous disdain.

His blue suit was severe and terribly correct, as were the white shirt with French cuffs showing modestly, the plain grey tie, the squared white handkerchief. He had the falsely smug look of a man who would be totally unarmed without the weapon of position.

His eyes merely touched his brother with a quick speculative glance. "'Lo, Bryan," he said, without offering his hand. "Mother, why have you told Bryan? Why is he here? I thought this was strictly a fam—that is, I thought you intended to keep the matter a careful secret."

"I'll answer that, Junior," said Bryan, who was partly amused because his brother was so ridiculous and partly irritated because Van was just the type of bastard who made life miserable for a lot of little people who couldn't afford to be so objective. "Mom didn't want to send a boy on a man's errand."

"Bryan! I didn't say that at all. I said—"

"So you can stop talking around me," Bryan interrupted, "I'm in—all the way."

Van sat down slowly and removed his glasses for no other apparent reason than to busy his hands. His face looked naked, a bright spot of colour touched his pale cheeks.

"Very well," he said. "I do think Father would want *me* to represent his interests. But since you don't need me, I'll run along. I have a great deal of work that I—"

"Oh, shut up," said Bryan without real anger.

"Stop it, just stop it!" Margaret Wyckoff commanded. "Both of you. There's no room for animosity here, no room for selfish ego. Now, Van, did you attend to the money?"

Van Wyckoff replaced the glasses fussily and suddenly his face became clothed.

"Yes," he said. "I sold the stock. We're in a nervous market right now, a lot of profit-taking this time of year, and then there's the war situation and—"

"Yes, yes, but you sold it?"

"Well, I couldn't wait for a price, that's all. So maybe I lost half a point." He produced a check and passed it to her. "If you'll sign this, I'll deliver it to the bank. I've alerted Bill McCallum and the cash is already being counted. We can pick it up at noon tomorrow—Six hundred thousand. Lord! These thugs have expensive tastes."

"All right," said Margaret Wyckoff, signing the check, returning it with Van's pen. "Did you talk with Harvey Burnett?" She turned to Bryan. "I just couldn't trust myself with Harvey. I was afraid I'd break down and give it away."

"Oh yes," Van answered. "I called Burnett. I told him that we were in touch with father, that he was all right but that he had been detained because of a family matter which was extremely delicate and personal and which he would explain himself at another time, that there was no reason at all for alarm."

"I suppose he was perfectly convinced and incurious," said Bryan.

"Well, no. He was mighty curious, even suspicious. But I'm sure he assumed it was an entirely different kind of thing. Ahhh—well, you understand."

"No," said Bryan innocently. "What kind of thing?"

Van glanced at his mother from the corner of his eye and was silent.

"Oh," said Bryan. "You mean, he thought the Old Man might be involved with some dame?"

"That's not exactly—"

"The train ticket," said Margaret Wyckoff. "Did you have time to check into the reservation?"

Van nodded. "It's done. I sent a messenger-for it. Richard C. Brown, Car A-153, Compartment B, 10.40 tomorrow night. I have it here in my pocket."

"I'll take it," said Bryan. "Unless of course you'd rather go yourself. In which case, I'd suggest carrying a gun. From the sound of the note, anything might happen. For instance, those hoods might grab you until they checked the money. And then, well—yes, I think you'd better be armed." He sat back and waited.

"Of course," said Van quickly, "I expected to be the one to go. But then I thought Mother decided ..." His voice trailed off.

After a moment Bryan extended his hand, and Van got up slowly and brought him the ticket.

"I'll be here at noon tomorrow," Bryan said, "for the money."

"Yes," said Van absently. Bending, he kissed his mother on the cheek. "I'll be getting back to the office. Call you later, dear. It's a dreadful thing—dreadful! But don't worry, I know he's going to be all right. I know we're going to pull him out of it."

"Are we?" said Bryan.

"Thank you, Van," said his mother, dabbing her eyes with a handkerchief. "You've been a big help, a very big help."

Van Wyckoff smiled magnanimously, moved to leave, then turned.

"This is an unexpected loyalty, Bryan. I want you to know that we're grateful."

Bryan puffed smoke and looked at his brother without answering. After an awkward silence, his brother turned again and departed.

"Why can't people love each other?" said his mother brokenly, when the door had closed. "Why can't everyone in the world be kind to one another?"

"I don't know," said Bryan. "But I'll ask Dad—the next time I see him."

CHAPTER FIVE

Somewhere in South Georgia. 6:10 P.M. Wednesday. Car A-153, Compartment B.

The streamliner burrowed into the night with an endless, dull rumble and thin clatter of wheels which was almost unvarying in pitch except as the roadbed flung over bridges. Then the sound was like thunder heard from a sealed room. Out of the darkness the whistle blast was a plaintive, lonely wail, echoing back from the countryside, dying on a note of despair.

Bryan Wyckoff slouched in his seat, his head twisted toward the window. He viewed the moon-pale blur of landscape with weary inattention, lulled by the stupid monotony of it—a stand of trees, a clearing, more trees; sagging shacks, a farm, a stretch of parallel highway; spaced dancing cones of light, a crossing. Then the pattern began again, over and over.

He was beat down by the waiting. A kind of anti-climactic fatigue had set in. Since New York, through all the states, there had been nothing, no sign of a contact. He had not left the compartment, that tiny cell in the prison of the train. The porter, his jailer, had brought him food with a whitewash of a smile splashed in ebony, the smile widening with a five-dollar bill.

Throughout the long hours he had not really slept. Listening, even in the dark, for that signal knock at his door which never came. The door was always kept locked. And when a knock came, even when he knew it must be the porter, he answered with a tight grip on the .32 automatic in his pocket. Not that he intended some foolish bravado, but there might be hidden factors of the scheme, laden with danger—and you could not leave a suitcase containing thousands of dollars unguarded!

There had been too much time for thinking, most of it destructive. It was becoming more difficult to believe that they would really let the Old Man go free, even after a payment of over half a million. For what? So that he could unfold a dozen clues to aid the police? Oh, no. Not with kidnapping a crime which could be punished by death in New York, a life sentence in Florida.

Yet there was one hope. They probably wanted to keep his father alive until after the money changed hands. He would still be useful as a bargaining tool until then. And with this in mind, Bryan had developed a plan of his own. It was risky. Yet no other plan he could come by contained an ounce of insurance.

But now he was immeasurably depressed. Why should the contact wait so long? Something must have gone wrong. Whatever the plot, it must have collapsed in fear of a train stacked with plainclothes police. And perhaps, at the last moment, the contact panicked, dropped off at some station long ago. Because whatever the gimmick, it could have seemed workable in theory, impossible in practice.

But this was pure speculation, wasted energy. He was drained by it. He picked up the book he had been reading and after a few false starts, finally got lost for a chapter. He began another and promptly fell asleep.

The sound crept upon his consciousness. Then his eyes snapped open. Silence. If someone had been knocking, he had stopped.

Standing, Bryan glanced at his watch. He had slept only fifteen minutes. He moved to the door. The sharp tapping came precisely as he inclined his head to listen. It was not a secretive or fearful sound. The porter? No. He had finished dinner, the dishes had been removed.

He got a grip on the gun in his pocket, opened the door.

"Mr. Brown?" the girl said. "Mr. Richard C. Brown?"

"That's right."

"I have something for you." Opening her purse, she produced a small package which she handed to him.

She had one of those cool, bland faces which at first seems passive, wooden, and then surprises with a sudden
expression. A mature face with a look of reserve and capability not often acquired in the mid-twenties. She had chestnut hair with straight bangs and gentle waves which settled just above the shoulders. A slim nose was slightly hooked above a rich soft mouth and a firm little chin. Slanting green-grey eyes gave the impression of stillness which is sometimes the veil of turmoil.

Spiked heels and a lifting posture made it difficult to judge accurately, but she did not appear excessively tall. She wore a plain, black wool sheath. The dress was smart and also subtle. It merely hinted at bold breasts above a long trim waist and lush thighs.

Watching her, Bryan opened the package. It was wrapped in thin, grey paper of the type used in drugstores, corded with white string. The paper covered a plain white box. The box contained a gold watch in a diamond-shaped case. Even before he turned it over and read the inscription, Bryan recognised it as his father's.

Bryan stared coldly at the girl. She no longer seemed attractive. She grew loathsome and cunning under his gaze.

"You'd better come in," he said. "We can't talk here."

Her raised eyebrows indicated a slight annoyance.

"I think you misunderstand," she said. "There was a gentleman in the club car. We got to talking. He asked me if I would deliver the package to you."

"Well, why didn't this guy come himself?"

"He said he wanted it to be a little surprise gift for you to open after he was gone. He got off at the last stop."

"Oh yeah? What was the man's name?"

"He didn't say. I only talked to him for a minute. But there's supposed to be a card inside."

He looked and there was—in a sealed, white envelope. He opened it. The message was typed.

> Go to car A-150, Room D. Be quick! The door is open. Leave the money and return immediately to your own compartment. Remain there for not less than thirty minutes.
>
> Don't try anything clever. You'll be watched!

"What did this man look like?" said Bryan, tucking the card in his pocket.

"Don't you even know him? Isn't the card signed?" she said impatiently.

"No. I'm afraid not."

"Well, this is simply ridiculous!" She frowned. "I don't see how there could be a mistake. He gave your name and told me where to find you. I'm sorry I got into this, just doing the man a favour."

"Sure. That's the way it goes. Now just tell me what the man looked like."

"Well, he was around forty, I'd say. He was smallish and—and heavy. He had very black, straight hair. He had a rather bulbous nose and a wart, just here, at the corner of his left eye."

"Nothing else?"

She touched a long tapered forefinger to her brow, concentrating. She looked up suddenly. "Listen, is there anything wrong? Somehow you make me feel there's something wrong about this whole business."

"Naturally, I'm curious," he evaded. "Try to think, now."

"Well, he had dark skin, a little pocked. And he had a very, very slight accent. I couldn't place it. He spoke softly, he was extremely courteous, otherwise—don't you know him at all? I got the impression he had been with you on the train."

"What was the station? Where he got off."

"As I said, the last stop—Savannah. Now really, Mr. Brown, I have to go."

Bryan studied her. The innocent traveller making delivery? Such a neat, safe method of contact—it had never occurred to him.

"What's your name?" he asked.

"Does it matter?"

"Not particularly."

"I think you're extremely rude." She looked him carefully in the eye. Then she turned to leave.

"Wait," he said. "I'm sorry."

She paused, looked over her shoulder.

"I'm under a strain," he said. "A beaut. And I can't explain why. It's something personal. Thanks for bringing the package, whoever sent it. I realize that you're just caught in the middle." He smiled.

She came back a step. "That's perfectly all right."

"You see, there may be more to this than appears on the surface, Miss …"

"Russell. Pauline Russell."

"How far are you travelling, Miss Russell?"

"All the way to Miami."

"Good. Now I wonder if you could tell me where to find you on the train in case I need to ask you another question about this?" He held up the package.

"As long as you don't use it as a springboard," she said. "Because I'll tell you frankly that I'm not interested in train-games, cocktails and chit-chat, progressing to minor amour. I have my own problems."

"At any other time I'd be mighty disappointed." He grinned. "But I meant just what I said, no more."

"In that case, I'm riding coach. Just walk forward until you spot me."

"Thanks again, Miss Russell."

She waved and he stepped back into the compartment, locking the door. The train thundered over a bridge and gathered speed.

He looked again at the watch and the note. Then he got the small grey suitcase from beneath the seat and opened it. Green bundles nudged each other in orderly rows. He leafed through one of the bundles to make certain he had not forgotten to place, at centre, the note which contained his demand. It was there. He closed the case and unlocking the door, carried the money to Car A-150.

He found Room D and hesitated, peering up and down the passageway. Then, the hand in his pocket around the gun, he opened the door and went in.

The room was empty—no clothing or luggage about, not a trace of anyone. He set the suitcase on the seat and left, closing the door.

He noticed that the door to one of the rooms nearby had been opened and that a man sat reading a newspaper. The man's face was hidden behind the paper. Well, a small invisible hole could be punched in a newspaper, just large enough for limited observation ...

Bryan paused at the end of the car, wondering if he should chance a minute to see what, if anything, happened next. Obviously someone was going to enter that room for the money, and probably that person wouldn't wait very long.

But when a minute passed without incident, he decided not to jeopardize the exchange. He went back to his compartment and checked his watch to time out the thirty minutes. One thing was evident, no one would jump off a train travelling close to seventy miles an hour. The contact wasn't going anywhere for a while.

The contact—were there two? Logically, if the man who gave Pauline Russell the package got off at Savannah, there had to be two! One man gives her the watch and gets off immediately, so that even if she has a description, he can't be located. A second man remains on the train. The contact job has been done for him. He has but to pick up the money from Room D. But how does he do this without the risk of being observed? Ahhh, there's the puzzle, thought Bryan. Perhaps he amply gambles that there are no police aboard.

Not likely—the plan was too careful. Well, it made no difference. Whatever the dodge, it wouldn't affect his own scheme.

But in fifteen minutes, when the train pulled into Jacksonville, he guessed the next move. The contact man would get off here with the money and disappear!

Bryan decided to take a chance. With the gun in his hand he draped his trench coat over his arm so that the automatic was concealed. He left the compartment and got off the train. A porter told him he would have ten minutes. He walked quickly ahead until he came to a freight-loading cart piled high with mail sacks. He stood behind the cart, watching the passengers detrain and walk toward the exit. He was looking for the small grey suitcase with the money. When he found the case, he would find his man.

Instead, he spied Pauline Russell moving briskly toward the exit. Now and then she glanced back over her shoulder. She seemed in a frantic hurry. She carried a blue overnight case. Bryan knew she had transferred the money.

As she was about to pass he stepped out in front of her, blocking the way.

"I thought you were going to Miami, Miss Russell," he said. "Why did you lie to me unless you had something to hide?"

Her mouth fell open. She tried, but couldn't find words.

"There never was a chubby little man with a wart under his eye," said Bryan. "You were the contact all the time."

"Get out of my way!" she said. "Or—or I'll call for help."

"Why don't you do that?" he asked. "See if you can raise a policeman, while you're at it. I'll help you. No? Then get back on that train and we'll have a little talk—all the way to Miami."

"No," she said, "I won't." Her jaw became set, her eyes sullen. "You can't make me, either." She attempted to go around him.

He side-stepped, said, "Take a look at this." He showed her the gun beneath the coat. "And then change your mind. Okay, move!

Right back on the train, sister. After you."

He gave her a little shove in front of him and they climbed aboard. He steered her through the cars to his compartment They went in and he locked the door. He pulled the shade down over the window.

"Now, Pauline, have a seat right there. And don't think because you're a woman you can lie to me again. Before we reach Miami, I'm going to have the truth." He lifted her chin with the barrel of the gun. "One way or another," he said.

CHAPTER SIX

Bryan put the automatic in his pocket She had set the blue overnight case on the floor beside her and now he hoisted it to the seat and reached for the catch.

"What're you doing?" she said. "That's mine! You have no right to touch it."

It was a good act. She seemed genuinely outraged. He ignored her and opened the case—a folded dress, a pair of panties and a bra, stockings, nightgown. He searched underneath—a book, a comb and brush, the usual cosmetics. He closed the case and looked at her steadily. With a little jolt the train began to move.

"What did you do with the money, Pauline?"

"Money? I don't know what you're talking about." Her eyes had regained their icy calm, her face was like a stone. "If it's money you want, I have about a hundred dollars. Take it and let me go."

He grabbed her purse from her lap, opened it. In a billfold there were five new twenties and some ones, assorted credit cards, a driver's licence. He studied the licence.

"Your real name is Pauline Ingram," he said, "not Russell. Another lie. You live in Miami Beach and you claim to be a photographer. Interesting. What do you photograph, twenty-dollar bills?"

She was silent. She-wore a look of fixed defiance, as if she had been told that when the chips were down, nothing must move her to say anything of value to the enemy.

He put the licence back and returned the purse. A train whooshed by in the other direction. Air currents made the window tremble. The clatter ceased and he sat down, facing her.

"What were you going to do?" he said. "Meet somewhere in Jacksonville for the split?"

She said nothing, but he saw that her hands were tightly clenched.

"Listen, you evil bitch," he aimed a finger at her, "I haven't decided how I'm going to open you up, but it's a long way to Miami and we won't be disturbed. So make up your mind to play it on the level. You've got about one minute before the game gets rough."

She looked at him and saw that he meant it. A small shadow of doubt crossed her face.

"What have I ever done to you?" she said.

"The trouble with my Old Man, he likes women too much, Pauline. I have a hunch you sexed him into a trap, and that's how he was kidnapped."

Her face slowly unravelled, became incredulous. "Kidnapped? Your father was kidnapped?"

"Aw, come on now, Pauline. Put away the act. I'm convinced you've got talent."

"If you're serious," she said, "you've got the wrong person. I don't know anything about it."

Her eyes were dilated with wonder. It was difficult not to believe her.

"I'll tell you what, Pauline. I wouldn't enjoy having to maul you—I might not have the stomach for it—so I'll tell you a secret Your accomplice is going to count that money soon. And he's going to find there's only a hundred thousand and a little note explaining the absence of the other half million I kept out to bargain with. You see, I know your kind. I know that once you have all the money, Floyd Cameron Wyckoff is a dead man. So I kept the big chunk in reserve. They'll have to let me talk to him first. Then I'll stall while the money is supposedly being transferred to a Miami bank, though by this time it's already on deposit. That'll give me a couple of days to find those bastards, you see?"

"No," she said in a hushed voice, "I don't see at all. Who are you, anyway?"

"Now what I want to do, Pauline, is to make a deal with you. I'll give you a hundred thousand cash tomorrow morning—for the right information. Then I'll let you have a couple of hours' head start before I turn you in. Otherwise—well, there's no choice. I'll just hand you over to the police the minute we arrive in Miami. Now, which will it be?"

"Let me get this straight," she said in a breathy voice, full of emotion. "Your real name is Wyckoff and your father has been kidnapped, is that it?"

"Oh, you're catching on. You've just said your first words of truth." He grinned wryly.

"And what does the watch have to do with it, the one I delivered in the package?"

She was leaning toward him intently, her face, a picture of startled innocence. He kept smiling back at her, wanting to smash his hand across her cheek.

"I think I understand now." She nodded slowly. "The watch belonged to your father, and I was the goat. They were just using me."

"Good try, Pauline. A hundred thousand dollars, Pauline, and freedom—two hours' start."

"Mr. Wyckoff," she said earnestly. "I'd do most anything in the world for a hundred thousand dollars, anything legal. But I'm no criminal. I've never been near a jail. There are a dozen people who will vouch for me. And this is the very first I knew of a kidnapping."

"A hundred thousand isn't enough, Pauline? A cross is risky? You could get killed? All right, we'll come to terms. How much do you want? Convince me that you know the hiding place, and you can practically make your own deal. All I want is to insure my father's safety."

"Listen," she said. "I couldn't tell you for a million. I don't know anything at all and never did. Will you at least hear my story?"

"No."

"Why not? You said yourself, we have plenty of time. What've you got to lose? If you don't believe me, then I'll be glad to tell the police."

Now he was not quite so certain. Why shouldn't she want the money? He got a cigarette going and sat frowning, really afraid that she might, after all, be telling the truth. Then what?

"I'm listening, Pauline."

"Could I have a cigarette, too?"

He gave her one and lighted it. She exhaled toward the window and turned back.

"I was one of those girls who takes your picture in night clubs," she said. "Until a couple of weeks ago, I was working at a place

called the Sultan's Tower. It's a rooftop night spot at one of the hotels on the beach—dancing, a
view. I was working for a man who paid me a salary and a percentage. He had a little dark room and while I clicked, he developed. It was a good thing, but it was too cozy from the beginning. I had a crush on this man and we were—uh—well, we were supposed to get married. And then I found out he lied to me. He was already married. And further, he had no intention of getting a divorce. So I quit."

She dragged deeply and touched her temple with fluttering fingers.

"I was in a grim state of mind—couldn't sleep, couldn't eat. But I could drink. Oh, how I could drink! I was coming apart like Shredded Wheat and it reached a point where I would have done almost any crazy thing just for distraction. Besides, I was set up in an expensive apartment, living week-to-week in a style that chewed up everything I earned.

"One morning I read an ad in the newspaper. I can repeat it word for word: 'Wanted. Attractive young woman to train for government agency position. Fascinating career. Expense-paid travel in U.S. No experience necessary. Must be intelligent, responsible type able to furnish excellent personal references. Salary unlimited to right person.'

"The ad sounded rather intriguing and there was a chance to get out of town, and I was so very anxious to get out of Miami for just a little while. There was a telephone number and a name, Mildred J. Talbot. I called the number and got an answering service. I was told to leave my name and a phone where I could be reached. Mrs. Talbot would call me in the early evening since she was going to be in conference all day.

"I didn't expect to hear from her, but sure enough about six, she was on the line. She asked me a great many questions about myself, all very pleasant and tactfully put, but thorough. She told me the job would require that I be sent on some highly secret, but not dangerous, missions for a new branch of the government's Central Intelligence Agency, and that I could earn as high as a thousand a month after a period of trial and probation. She asked for references and took them down as I dictated, said she would call back in an hour if she thought she would like to arrange a personal interview."

Pauline Ingram paused, as if waiting for comment. Bryan was silent, his face stern, offering her nothing.

"Well," she continued, "I knew this Mildred Talbot was checking because one of the people I had given her as a reference called me in about twenty minutes. He wanted to know what was going on, all these questions about my character—honesty, reliability and so on. Then Talbot herself phoned. She said the C.I.A. was just then setting up an office in town and she had come ahead from Washington to scout two local females as agents for what she called a special cell. She said everything was disorganized at the office; the phones hadn't even been installed. Since she was pressed for time the next day, could I meet her in an hour for a drink and a chat at the Dupont Plaza?

"So I went over there. And I was impressed. She was a crisp, fine-looking woman about forty-five or fifty. She was tall, wore glasses, had grey-streaked blonde hair. She had a very slight Southern accent She was as sharp and cool as an icicle—a very dominant type, but pleasant, you know. She asked more about my background, took notes.

"She said they needed someone in a hurry for an assignment but that she couldn't tell me a thing until I had been given the routine security check, and even then, I would have to be able to follow instructions to the letter without asking questions. Finally, she wanted to know if I would be available at a moment's notice if, in a few days, a decision was made in my favour. I said of course, and we parted with the understanding that she would be in touch, although other applicants were being considered.

"Well, damned if I didn't get another call from her the following Tuesday. I had been selected. Could I be ready to mond, Virginia, late that afternoon for a minor assignment, a sort of trial run? She would meet me at the airport with instructions, tickets and two hundred and fifty dollars advance pay. I would receive another two-fifty when I returned Wednesday, providing I was successful.

"I was terribly excited by the time I reached the airport—and just a little scared. But over a drink in the bar she explained that all I had to do was to deliver a package to a man on the Miami train and make note of his reactions. Then get off in Jacksonville and fly the rest of the way to make my report. The man's name was Richard C. Brown."

Bryan nodded in silence.

"Don't you believe me?"

"Who gave you that description of the guy with the wart under his eye?"

"She did. Oh, very carefully. I was rehearsed. Talbot said the description fitted a known Communist agent perfectly."

"You didn't question any of this?"

"Just once I said, 'Why?' and Mrs. Talbot snapped back that I was never again to ask the why of anything, just do as I was told. But she would allow me to know this much—that Richard C. Brown, an alias, was one of their own men, that he was suspected of leaking information to Communist agents, that this was a test. By his reaction it would be known if he was loyal."

"So you got on the train at Richmond?"

"Yes."

"You rode in the coach?"

"No. That was a lie. I had a roomette *in* the next car. But I was ordered to conceal everything about, myself including my name. I was supposed to get off at Jacksonville in order to avoid further contact with you."

"Why was there such a long delay in delivering the package after you boarded at Richmond?"

"I don't know. I was instructed to wait until a half-hour before we arrived in Jacksonville. But I was also told that if there was a change in plans, somehow a message would reach me."

"The time might have been used to case the train for police," said Bryan. "You knew nothing about a delivery of money to Room D, Car 150?"

"Nothing. This is the first I've heard of it."

"Or that there might be another so-called agent like yourself aboard?"

"No. I believed I was alone."

"It's just possible," Bryan mused, "that there was another sucker like you. Assuming there were two hired goats, one would make contact, the other would pick up the money and detrain at Jacksonville. If something went wrong and the police closed in, they'd have only a couple of dupes and a blind alley. Clever. Pretty goddamn clever."

"Then you do believe me?"

"Yes." He smiled. "I believe you. But I'm going to hang onto you anyway, just in case. Now, do you have an address where you were supposed to report to this Talbot woman?"

"No. She said it was best for me to stay away from the office because she didn't want any new agent to be known by an old one until this leak had been discovered. She said for me to go straight home and she would call me."

"That was so you wouldn't check on her for a day or so. Unless I'm way off, you'll never hear from her again. Tell me, didn't you once suspect something? Didn't the arrangements seem to be handled just a bit informally for a Government agency?"

"Yes and no. The cloak and dagger atmosphere seemed natural to someone like me, and this woman kept me on the defensive all the time. It was always *me* who was being checked. Then, too, I was never sure until the last minute that I was hired. I wasn't going to investigate a job that might never be a reality, anyway. You see? And by the time I was accepted, it was too late to do anything but pack and run."

"That was part of the strategy," said Bryan. He got up and lifted the window shade. For a moment he watched the shadowy terrain escape in the night. Then he removed his father's watch from his pocket and showed it to her along with the ransom note. For a few minutes he explained the details of the kidnapping.

"C'mon," he said afterwards. "Let's go have a look at Room D, Car 150. Might be something there."

Room D was empty. But they discovered what turned out to be a connecting door. Bryan had tried it the first time, but it was locked. Now it was open. It led to Room C—Empty. The porter said yes, there had been a nice young lady in Room C. No, she was not carrying a small grey suitcase. She had gotten off at Jacksonville. She had bought two tickets, one for her brother in Room D, but he had missed the train and the littlo lady was upset about it. "Yes, suh, she surely was!"

"I wonder," said Bryan when they had returned to the compartment, "what she did with that suitcase? Anyway, there you have just about all the pieces of the puzzle."

"Yes," said Pauline. "All but the most important ones. Who are they, and where are they holding your father?"

CHAPTER SEVEN

During the ride from the Miami airport, Norma DiNardo could hardly take her eyes from the small green case beside her in the taxi cab. This was partly because the case and the details surrounding her possession of it were a fascinating mystery, and partly because looking down at it sitting there on the floor of the cab it seemed almost alive, breathing menace with every fragile heartbeat.

Mrs. Talbot had told her that the bag would be perfectly safe to carry as long as it wasn't jostled about too roughly. But on the other hand, to tamper with the lock, and especially to lift the lid, would cost Norma her life. The highly secret content of the case was protected from falling into "enemy hands" by a device which set off an explosion the moment the case was opened, a kind of booby trap. Only an expert of the C.I.A. would be able to deactivate the bomb. Not even Mrs. Talbot herself understood the mechanism.

Originally, this invaluable piece of luggage had been grey. But, as instructed, Norma had quickly re-covered it with the deep green, plastic strips provided for the purpose, cutting them to size and gluing them in place just as she had practised it. Norma was made to understand that the case must be disguised because a C.I.A. agent who had knowledge of it was under suspicion of having defected to the Communists. Norma had been hired as a courier because she was unknown to the suspected agent. Thus he could not pass her description to an accomplice.

Norma was told that the bag would be brought aboard the train during the stop in Washington, but where it was going after she delivered it to Miami was forbidden knowledge.

At the prescribed time, she had opened the connecting door to Room D, removed the prize to C and, trembling a little, covered it quickly in the green plastic. The rest had been quite simple—off at Jacksonville, out to the airport, then the swift flight to Miami.

Norma might never have undertaken such a mission, even

though it was for her own government and she was reasonably patriotic. But the thought of earning five hundred dollars practically overnight, with more to come from future assignments, increased her patriotism enormously. She had quit her forty-five dollar a week typing job at the Sunkool Awning Company the same day she got the nod of approval from Mrs. Talbot.

She was a smallish girl of twenty-seven with short, dark hair and plain, unexciting features relieved somewhat by a wide, full-cushioned mouth. In manner, she appeared extremely docile. Underneath, she was churning with rebellion. She was an energetic person, covertly nervous, chronically irritated by the drabness of an existence which never matched the fanciful adventures of her imagination. She was a nail-biter, and occasionally her dark skin erupted in pimples which she covered with frantic applications of pancake.

While her face was unremarkable, a tempting figure earned a certain forgiveness. She had once been married and divorced.

Norma laid her hand, very gently, on the handle of the case as the cab came to rest before the portals of Dupont Plaza. The driver offered to take the bag but she refused on the grounds that it was light (true enough) and after paying the fare, reluctantly gave him a ten-cent tip.

She moved quickly across the lobby and found an elevator. Just as the door was about to close a tall, thickly built man in a slate-blue suit got aboard. There was an abrupt demanding maleness about him. Though he was not good-looking by any of the usual standards, Norma felt a soft tug of desire at the sight of him. As he turned about without a glance, there seemed something vaguely familiar about the shape of the back of his head. Under the present critical circumstances, since she did not know the man at all, she found the impression disturbing.

The car rose. She clutched the handle of the suitcase.

She got off at nine. The man had preceded her. She hesitated, then went past him down the corridor at just under a run. She did not look back until she had reached the door and knocked, loudly and repeatedly. The man was down a ways, diagonally across the corridor. He was standing before a door, casually removing a key from his pocket with his back turned. He wore no hat and the shape of his head was clear.

It came to her just as Mrs. Talbot opened the door. The man had been on the plane, two seats forward of her. Norma had a shrewd eye for men and she had been curious, but he had not once turned toward her.

"What's the matter?" said Mrs. Talbot. "You look positively grey, my dear!"

She stepped in before answering, set the case down gingerly, sighed with the sound of the door closing.

"I think I recognized a man in the elevator. He got off on this floor. I'm quite sure he was on the plane from Jacksonville."

"That's possible," said Mrs. Talbot, nodding and smiling faintly. "Our people were instructed to watch over you. There was a friendly agent near at all times. Certainly, if the man was not one of ours, you'd never have made it safely to my door." The smile faded, she stood tall and stern. "Now you must remember not to panic, Norma. We can't Bave that, you know. A good agent is cool and steady, even in danger."

"Im sorry, Mrs. Talbot." *The bitch!*

"Never mind. This is your first alignment and you did well, dear, very well, indeed." She drew deeply on a cigarette in a jewelled holder, adjusted her harlequin glasses, behind which her eyes shone with the same brilliance as sunshine refracted from ice. There was a prim handsomeness about her that made her brittle manner all the more annoying to Norma.

"Well, you must be tired, Norma. It's been a strain. No problems to report? Any strangers try to make conversation with you?"

"I didn't talk to a soul."

"No one appeared to follow you?"

"Only the man on the elevator, and that might have been a coincidence."

Mrs. Talbot's eyes dropped, as if in sudden memory, to the green case. "I'll just take this into the other room and then we'll reward a job well done, hmmm?"

"Yes, ma'am. I could use it, all right."

"I'm sure Now have a seat, Norma dear. I won't be a minute."

The things you do for money, Norma thought, as the green bag moved with Mrs. Talbot across the sitting room and into a bedroom *oat* of sight around the corner. But so broad was Norma's imagination and so intense her curiosity, she might even have relinquished the rest of her pay for a peek into the suitcase. *How silly, because even Mrs. Talbot couldn't —*

Norma heard a sharp little sound. She placed it immediately with a shock that stirred her anger—it was the sound of a spring latch snapping, the opening of a suitcase. She had been deceived! That woman had tricked her as if she were a stupid little girl!

On tiptoe she raced across the room and peered around the corner. The bedroom door was pushed to, but not closed. There was an inch or two of space in which she could see Mrs. Talbot's back. With a heart that nearly thundered in her ears, Norma inched forward until she could see clearly.

Talbot had set the case upon the bed and was leaning over it. The cover had been lifted and there was a partial view of the interior.

Money! What piles of it!

Talbot's fingers raced over the bills, picking up one bundle, dropping it for another. Then she plucked five bills from the top of a wad, folded them in her hand, closed the case.

Norma flew back to the chair, arranged her dress and her face into lines of composure.

Mrs. Talbot advanced with the bills, her bright eyes unsuspecting.

"Here we are, my dear—two hundred fifty, to make a total of five hundred, as promised."

Norma took the five fifty-dollar bills. "Thank you, Mrs. Talbot."

"I'll have another assignment for you, Norma, in a week or two. Meantime, I'm expecting some papers from Washington that you must fill out and sign to give you an official status. You'll be on the payroll and hereafter you'll be paid by check. Now I'll be in touch with you soon. Don't leave town and don't be away from home more than twelve hours at a stretch. Understand?"

"I think so."

"You think so?"

"I mean, yes, I—I understand." *Bitch!*

"And you are not to try to contact me—for reasons of security. I'll call or, if necessary, send someone."

"Yes, Mrs. Talbot. I'll remember."

Norma left as quickly and gracefully as possible, hurried by her knowledge. In the lobby she saw the same mail in the blue suit now buying a paper at a news-stand. She hastened out the door and, after a moment's hesitation, made for the parking lot in front of the hotel. It was dark enough and she hid behind a car.

Surprisingly, the man did not follow. She decided to wait a few minutes and see if he came out. She might even follow *him*. Norma was now convinced he was connected with Talbot and there was something weird going on. She had been lied to, she was a dope. *They* might be the Communists. All that money! It could be the payoff for stolen secrets. Why not? To think that she might uncover a whole network of spies, her picture in the paper beneath the headlines, her name a national byword. Norma DiNardo simply smothered in a tight circle of admixing officials, among them some wealthy and also charming bachelors!

The great parking lot was unattended, an area in shadow. But still, Norma did not like standing in the open. She moved around among the cars until she found a door unlocked and climbed in. While she watched, she fingered the fifty-dollar bills and created an imaginary future in fragmentary pictures, one of which even took her to the White House where she was honoured by the President.

Time passed swiftly. But when the man did not appear, she became restless. She had almost decided to leave when she saw him coming right toward the parking lot, carrying what probably was the green case, because stepping briskly beside him was Mrs. Talbot.

It looked as if they were moving which she was hiding, so she scrunched down and prayed. But then, when she peered out cautiously, they had turned to the left, their backs retreating in the darkness.

She got out and followed, ducking behind cars en route. She was going to try to get their licence number. She had them in sight, then lost them. She crouched down, darting forward in frenzied spurts.

There was the motor sound, just before lights flared twenty feet ahead. Norma leapt back instantly. Was she fast enough? Could they have seen her? All thought but escape left her. She fled between cars, hurtling herself toward the hotel. She didn't look back until she was almost there.

Nothing—they had gone.

Trembling, she approached the doorman and ordered a taxi.

"I'll have one for you Just in a minute, Miss," he said.

She stood biting her nails. She felt as if a rash were creeping over her body. She opened her purse and removed a comb, fussed with her hair in the back-flap mirror. She saw lights blaze up the drive and made ready to enter the cab.

"Norma! What on earth are you doing there?"

It wasn't a cab, it was Mrs. Talbot leaning from the window of a grey sedan, a Dodge. The man in the blue suit was at the wheel.

"Oh, hello, Mrs. Talbot," she said with all the ease she could muster. "I was just waiting for a taxi."

"In the parking lot?"

"What parking lot, Mrs Talbot?" The rash crept over the skin at the back of her neck.

"Norma dear, there is only *one* parking lot."

"I just thought I'd take a taxi," she repeated dumbly.

"But you left me at least twenty minutes ago."

"Yes, that's true," her lips froze in a sick smile. "Well, I was just exhausted from everything—you know. And I stopped for a drink in the bar."

"Really, Norma, we'll have to have a little talk. Now you get right in and we'll take you home where you belong."

The man had come around to open the back door of the Dodge. He seemed larger, more formidable than in the elevator. A small polite smile and the gesture of his hand invited her to the rear seat, but his eyes were a command.

"You're very kind," said Norma, half turning to the doorman, "but I've already sent for a taxi."

"No problem at all," said Mrs. Talbot blandly. "Cancel it."

"It's okay, Miss," said the doorman. "I didn't flag no cab yet. They're all busy."

With which, the man in the blue suit made an even broader gesture, mockingly magnanimous, toward the rear seat.

Norma felt numb, immobilized. Mentally, she got in the car and rode away. Physically, she stood perfectly still, reaching for a light in the dark pocket of her imagination.

"Well, I'll tell you," she said. "This is awfully nice of you, awfully nice—but I have a confession to make. Yes," her voice became confidential as she bent toward Mrs. Talbot, "a little confession. You see, I didn't really want a taxi and I don't need a lift home. Because I—it's terribly embarrassing—I made a date with a man, a gentleman—in the bar. He went to his room to change. And then we're going out on the town."

Mrs. Talbot and Blue-Suit exchanged looks. Suddenly, Mrs. Talbot began to chuckle in her throat, the sound rising to a brittle laughter that was apparently so infectious her companion joined in, drowning her out, wiping invisible tears from the corners of his eyes.

"Oh really," said Mrs. Talbot when they had subsided. "That's one of the best I've ever heard, the very best. It deserves a medal. You poor girl." Her voice had an edge of sarcasm which was lost upon Norma. "For heaven's sake, why didn't you come right out with it in the first place! Never mind." She smiled benignly. "Run along with your little friend and have a perfectly marvellous time. You deserve it. Doesn't she deserve it, Mr. D.? She certainly does." Her features returned to austerity. "But remember, now. You have your obligations and there are things you must never discuss. In that sense, you're always on duty."

"I'll remember," Norma answered, smiling her relief.

The man bowed—rather gallantly, she thought—then climbed behind the wheel. Mrs. Talbot waved cheerfully as they drove off.

Norma watched the grey deck, the red wink of tail lights, until the Dodge was out of sight.

I could be wrong, she thought. *Yes, I'm sure of it. They seem such friendly people. And someday I'll understand about the money.*

Nevertheless, she had made note of the licence number, saying it again and again to herself, and when she finally got into a cab, she wrote the number on an envelope.

She gave the driver her address. But when she was almost home she felt a wrench of loneliness in the vacuum of spent excitement. She had the cabby stop while she dialled a familiar number.

She came back with a complacent little smile and gave the driver a new address.

CHAPTER EIGHT

It was night. The room was stuffy because the windows were closed, also the door, sealing him in. The blinds had been drawn tight and the darkness was complete. There was a feeling of slow suffocation. And though the room was not really hot, Floyd Wyckoff lay in a constant sweat. Surprisingly, the chains which bound him to the bed were not too painful. There was just enough leeway to move the limbs for circulation.

The walls of the house were paper-thin and it was possible to hear fragments of conversation, especially from the living room. The voices accentuated his loneliness and despair, for they spoke of him dispassionately, with a subhuman detachment as emotionless as the blade of a scalpel.

Except in the most abstract sense, he did not even know where he was—somewhere in the south-western outskirts of the city, a small, insignificant white house in a section where other houses were scarce, perhaps on the edge of a farming district. He had no idea. He had paid so little attention. It wasn't important then, and a growing intuition told him it might never be important—not to him.

For the first time in years, perhaps twenty, he was aware of Ms own fraility in the face of disaster. How small a man grew when physical force could make him prisoner in an instant, when brute force, exerted by the dregs of humanity, could confront him with his own mortality. Where was that power which he had so recently wielded behind the bastions of social strata, of finance, of possession? Gone, made silly and ineffectual in the face of those two equally persuasive weapons—a *AS* calibre automatic and a woman.

All his life he had thought of himself as a man of strong moral fibre—not a surface strength, but strength in depth, containing an unmovable determination, a will which destroyed opposition, because at the core of the man there was no flabby area of vulner-ability.

And now he cursed that one weakness which he had forgiven himself, which he had belittled as a kind of joke, just a chronic irritation inherited by the male sex—the need of a woman. Oh, how stupid to underestimate the hypnosis of a superbly attractive female. By his very nature, a truly vital man was born to be victim-ized by a woman sooner or later.

But that was no excuse. A man who had so much to lose, even his life, should be twice on guard.

Wyckoff heard movements beyond the door and cocked his head to listen. Only two remained to watch him now. Bonnie and the one she called her husband had gone off somewhere. These two who stayed behind had said little in the past hour, just a few terse, mumbled comments. Wyckoff could sense their tension, a waiting for something a crisis.

Now footsteps approached the door, paused, went away again.

He clenched and unclenched his hands, exercising them. He moved his feet. He breathed deeply, tried to relax. His energy had been depleted by the expense of a useless anger and self-condem-nation. His eyes felt puffed and gritty with the want of sleep. They had taken his watch and even with daylight there was no longer time. He lay in a coma of disorientation.

He had begun to lose touch with the reality of his former life and its complexities. He thought of little things—to walk free into a night of stars and taste the wine of a new air, to swim in a clean froth of surf, to take a warm bath, to shave the itching stubble (ahhh, how he used to hate the minor ordeal of shaving), to hear the distant minuscule sounds of a city from an open window, know the well-being of the second martini, enjoy the first smell and taste of rare roast beef an inch thick, luxuriate in a bed of downy pillows and silky sheets, and sleep in a dark velvet vacuum of forgetful-ness ...

How bored he had been with all the simplicities which melted into the background of existence, muddied and unappreciated with the guarantee of continuation unto surfeit. While now, if he could grasp his freedom, the small pleasures would be special, having a distinction and flavour he had never found in them, for now he un-derstood that without true appreciation, all of a man's possessions, real or intangible, are lost to him.

The phone was ringing in the other room—a sharp demanding sound, yet so familiar, so commonplace, a means of communication to the avenues of safety. How far, that instrument? Twenty feet? An impossible distance.

"Yeah? ... Sure, who else? ... No, no trouble. He's nice and cozy ... That right? Got here okay, huh? And no cops on the—... Well, sure, sure. You can't spot 'em all, but you gotta figure that by now—... I know, I know. What about the loot? ... Oh, sweet Jesus, man! Looks like what? ... Well, f'crissake, can't she count? ... Sure, sure. You're right. She had to get outta there and—... Yeah, yeah. So what'll we do with the collateral? Dispose? ... Mmmm ... You bet Way out and way down! Okay, Dug, in about thirty minutes. We'll get ready."

There was the sound of the receiver slapped hard into the cradle.

"That was Duggan. The loot's here. No cops tailing that he could spot. He had a peek in the case—bright green, man, all green!"

"Lovely, lovely!"

"Yeah, but he says it looks a little thin for six hundred grand."

"How come, how come?"

"How do I know, how come? It better be there—all of it! They couldn't even do a fast count. Had to beat it outta there. Haulin' tail for home right now. Well, that should wrap it. Neat, huh?"

"What about Wyckoff?"

"Dug says to get 'im set to travel. We'll put 'im to sleep and when he wakes up he'll be takin' a bath in the big tub, a hundred fathoms—straight down."

"So what's the rush?"

"What's the rush? F'crissake, we'll be gone from this burg in an hour. C'mon!"

The door opened and a swath of yellow light sliced across the bed. Wyckoff looked up and for a moment was blinded. Then he saw the man with the A5 in his hip pocket bend and begin to work with the chains. The other, with the hunting knife strapped to his belt, just stood gazing down, hands on hips.

Wyckoff peered into the man's face to find something, but was more frightened because there was nothing there at all—neither cruel pleasure nor animosity—but a simian vacancy.

CHAPTER NINE

"Well," said Pauline Ingram when Bryan had locked the door. "Isn't this cozy? I suppose you're going to keep me a prisoner in this hotel room all night."

"Who said you're a prisoner?" Bryan crossed to a window, heaved it open, peered down at the night traffic along Biscayne Boulevard. He had just registered at the Columbus and they had given him a room on the sixth floor.

"That gun in your pocket has been saying I'm a prisoner for quite awhile now." She sat on the edge of a chair and worked the catch of her purse nervously.

Bryan turned. "You just assumed that. Have I threatened you?"

"No. Not lately."

"Then forget it."

"In that case, I have my own apartment I'd just love to go home and get some sleep. It's after midnight."

"Go right ahead. Think of yourself, like all the other first-person slobs. Don't let the mere fact that a man's life is at stake this very moment keep you from your sleep."

She was silent. Then she said, "Well, of course I'll stay. That is, if I can be of any use. I know how much your father must mean to you."

"Oh, crap! He doesn't mean a thing to me." He sat down on a corner of the bed. "No more than any other total stranger, maybe less."

"You're not serious?" Her face was a small study in shock.

"Quite serious. We haven't spoken in years." She refused the cigarette he offered and he got one going for himself.

"If you really hate him so much, why do you bother?"

"My mother thinks he's great, and I'm very fond of my mother. Besides, I don't hate him. I just stopped caring about him one way or the other a long time ago. Maybe it's for the best. I can handle this with a certain detachment. Emotions have a way of fogging up good judgment."

She shifted in her chair, crossed her legs. Hands clasped around her knee, she leaned forward, studying him. It was an interesting face, he decided, now tranquil, now crisply alert, the eyes swiftly changing moods, the abundant mouth piquant and sensitive.

"You sound rejected," she said.

"By the Old Man? Sure, but it doesn't hurt any more. What you don't need can't hurt you. People I'm not able to come to terms with I've learned to cross out entirely instead of resenting them. Related or not, for me they simply cease to exist. Hell, there are only two or three persons in the whole world you can get to love in a lifetime, anyway. It isn't logical that one of those has got to be your Old Man. Then there's another half dozen you can enjoy well enough, providing you don't have to be locked in close company with them for more than two days at a time. In between there's nothing, just characters you wave to."

"You're bitter," she said.

"No, I think you're wrong. I'm reasonably cynical, but not bitter. Some people look at garbage and they see the shine of pure gold. I look at garbage and I see garbage. Period. If that's bitter, then I'm bitter."

"I'll take that cigarette now," she said. "Why did you break with your father, Mr. Wyckoff? Tell me it's none of my business, if you like."

"It's none of your business." He gave her a light. "But I'd tell you about it anyway if we had time. Listen, if you're going to stay more than five minutes, call me Bryan, will you?"

"How do you make your living … Bryan?"

"I worked hard until I was twenty-one, then I retired."

She laughed. "If I knew you better, I'd be terribly annoyed."

"If you knew me better, you wouldn't have to be annoyed. Now, let's get down to business. I want to pump you again for any little clue that might help. First I'll explain the situation in more detail. I left a note with the money as I told you. The note gives this hotel as the place to contact me, still using the name Richard C. Brown." He looked at his watch. "I might get a call anytime and until I do I'm going to stay put here."

"What does the note say exactly?"

"It explains how they get the rest of the money—on my terms. When they open that case and make a count, they'll find I've padded it with small bills. Half a million will be missing. In order to get that half million, they'll have to let me speak with the Old Man on the phone. And then they'll have to wait a couple of days for the money to be transferred from New York. I told them we couldn't raise over a hundred thousand on short notice. That's my story and it's a stall. I'm counting on their greed to give me more time to find the bastards. But if I can't run down the location in two days' time, it's pretty hopeless. I figure they'll kill him the minute they get their hands on all of the dough. And I guess they'll kill him anyway if I stall more than two days."

"What will you do," she asked, "if you can't find where they're holding him in time?"

"I'll demand an on-the-spot exchange, the cash for the man, any place they choose, however remote. It's a hundred-to-one they won't go for that. But there's an off-chance. If not, there's only the police. I don't know. I might work with the police anyway. It depends on finding a way to keep it quiet I haven't figured one yet. It's got to be foolproof."

"I don't envy you," she said. "Two days isn't long."

"Hell, no! That's why I've got to move fast. I don't dare stall for longer."

"But you think they'll accept the two-day wait?"

"They won't have a choice. I'm going to stand pat. It's a risk that's got to be taken. I explained in the note that raising the six hundred thousand without the help of my father was a big order and damn complicated. I told them I sent the hundred thousand to show good faith until the balance could be raised. If there's a real brain behind the thing, and obviously there is, that should satisfy. The wording of the ransom note, the whole scheme, indicates a pretty high level of intelligence. No half-wit conceived of this. By the same token, because so much preparation went into the plan, I have a strong hunch they intend to get six hundred thousand and not a cent less—that much is on our side."

She nodded. "Oh, they're not dumb. I'll vouch for that, if Talbot is a sample. In fact, the basic idea is brilliant."

"Sure Because in a kidnapping the one hitch, the real stumbling block, is the danger in taking possession of the ransom money. In spite of all his threats, at the point of exchange the kidnapper is most vulnerable. He can fall into a beautiful trap. The minute his grubby hands close on the money, cops in hiding can grab him, and he knows that. He can practically taste the fear of it. So much so, that a lot of times you read about how these birds got cold feet and didn't pick up the loot at all.

"So, how do you remove the element of risk? You hire a couple of innocent, and slightly gullible, stooges to do the dirty work for you. If they get caught, so what? They've been snowed. They don't really know a damn thing. They can tell the police nothing that will be of any real value. It's practically perfect. Still, I've got to find a hole somewhere."

She sat smoking reflectively, a small frown on her face.

"Suppose," she said, "the second girl, the girl in Room C, was one of them and I was the only dope."

"I don't believe it, Pauline. Remember that your friend Talbot said she was looking for a couple of girls, not just one. Besides, that would be inconsistent with the safety of the plan."

"Why girls, Bryan? Why not men?"

He shrugged. "Maybe because little girls are easier to fool with this C.I.A. hocus-pocus. They don't always have a man's logic. And maybe because a pretty girl on a train is not going to be as suspicious. Who's looking for a pretty girl in a kidnap plot?"

"Thanks," she said, "for the pretty girl part."

"It was the least I could do."

"All right, Bryan. Try this for logic—if the second girl is carrying the money, suppose she gets caught? You say she doesn't know anything, but she does. She has to know where to deliver the ransom. If the police grab her, the entire theory falls apart."

"I've been trying to puzzle that one, and I think I've got it. This second girl has a tail. Otherwise, what's to prevent her from just vanishing with the cash? The tail keeps her in sight at all times. If the cops nail her, he's going to be the first to get wind of it. So then, he calls ahead to the delivery point and he says, 'Scram, buddy! They pinched the girl.' The police arrive at the delivery point, but the bird has flown. See?"

"Yes. And you can just bet the bird would be Talbot."

"Sure. She's the only link, Pauline, unless you can tell me how to find the second girl."

"Well, I have one crazy idea."

"What's that?"

"Advertise. Something in the personal columns. Mildred J. Talbot seeking to contact female employee recently hired for government agency position. Urgent Phone—and then give her your own number."

"Very good! But I don't believe it would work. On the front page, yes, it might very well. In the personal columns, no, a thousand-to-one against it. How many people read through an entire paper, including the personal columns? Not unless they have a special reason for doing so. Nope, we'll have to find that girl some other way. And even if we can, she might not know much more than you do. But the place to start tracing her down would be the Dupont Plaza. Isn't that where this Talbot woman was staying when you met her?"

"Yes."

"She had a room there?"

"That's what she said."

"Then you were never in the room?"

"No. We talked in the cocktail lounge and she—"

The phone rang.

"That should be it!" said Bryan. "Now be quiet. Not a word!"

She nodded, sat tensely forward on the edge of her chair. Bryan lifted the receiver. "Yes?"

"You Richard Brown?" A man's voice,
right."

"Don't bother to trace, pal. I'm calling from a booth. You'd never make it."

"Don't worry—pal. I wasn't going to try."

"On this deal, friend, you stalling. You think you're playin' with kids? We got the big hand, fella. Ante up—tonight—or else!"

"No sale—friend! We've got cards, too. Half a million, all green. We settle Friday night, in two days. It can't be done sooner. So don't give me any pressure. It won't work."

"You want your boy squashed? Ten minutes from now we'll take 'im apart and send you the pieces."

"Go ahead. You want me to beg? You want me to cry? Sorry pal. No tears from me. I'm just the messenger boy, remember? Do what you want. I'll send flowers—or I'll make you rich. Take your choice. Friday night."

"We got a hundred grand. We could get along on that, wise guy."

"Then get along on it. Don't tell me your troubles. Friday night."

After a long silence. "Okay, Friday. We'll set it up tomorrow night. You wait for a call. Seven on the nose."

"I won't be here for that call, not unless you let me talk to the man."

"You'll talk to him. Like I said, seven, tomorrow."

The phone went dead. Bryan hung up, surprised to find that he was shaking.

"Well, Pauline," he said, "end of round one."

"Oh," she groaned. "The way you talked! You'd think your father was just so much—so much—"

"That's right, Pauline. That's right. Like he was so much meat for sale. And I had to think of him that way because you can't talk to those creeps in any other language. Let them hear so much as a frog in your throat, and the bargaining is over. I'm just glad I haven't set eyes on him in four years or I might never have carried it off.

"Now, c'mon. I've got two days and two nights and there won't be much sleep for me. Every minute counts. Let's get over to the Dupont and see if we can raise even a smell of Mildred J. Talbot."

CHAPTER TEN

Bonnie was undressing in the bedroom next to the room where they had Floyd Wyckoff chained. Larry, her husband, called Dug by the others, had gone out with Vince to make contact for the ransom. Only Brock remained. She could hear him pacing out there in the living room, working himself into a lather because he was worried, didn't like the way things were going.

Brock wanted to grab a share of the hundred grand and take off on his own, while she and Larry were still supremely confident they'd get the whole six hundred thousand. Vince would go with the majority because he seldom had an original thought. The idea of the baited trap was Larry's anyway, though she had given the plan her own special genius.

Vince and Brock were just a couple of goons, errand boys for Larry. They'd be damn glad to take fifty thousand apiece, leaving the sweet half million to Bonnie and her husband. But if it developed that there was a last-minute jealousy over the split, Larry would be ready for that too. Larry expected a cross from everyone, everywhere, and never left anything to chance.

Bonnie was sitting on the bed in panties and bra, fixing the long ebony strands of her hair into a pony tail. She had decided to change from a dress into slacks and a blouse, making herself generally as unfeminine as possible.

This was because Vince, and especially Brock, were a couple of uncaged monkeys who were incessantly watching her with sneaky, feral eyes, covertly speculating on the possibilities of her body. If she wasn't careful, that smouldering lust would catch fire, one of them would make a move and there would be a nasty fight which might upset the whole plan.

For her part; Bonnie didn't care. Vince and Brock were the sort of basic animals about whom she had only superficial knowledge. She was curious. Eternally she sought out larger and more dangerous thrills, especially those kicks which were sensual.

But while Larry was perfectly willing to sell her sex appeal for the kind of gain involved in the Wyckoff thing, he wasn't lending her to any of his friends. No, there could be a brutal fight and she must be careful. They would be sitting up till dawn discussing the change of plan, and it would be best for her to tone herself down, lessen temptation. Because, above all, Bonnie wanted that Big Money which would guarantee a cushion of splendour for the rest of her life.

She was a tall, slim-waisted, long-legged girl of twenty-nine with lusty, uptilted breasts. Except for a small, centre ridge of bone that somewhat spoiled her nose, she had nearly classic features which bore a look of haughty refinement This was partly an accident of nature and partly a re

self-image of a vast superiority. She had long ago decided that the world was full of idiots. She often said that most people were "too stupid to let live", and meant exactly that.

Hers was a sensual face, and yet a shrewdness about the eyes and mouth lessened its attraction. She was exceedingly clever, even brilliant. During her college years she had excelled in any study which pleased her, cheating at the boring junk with a cunning success.

She had a calculated charm which she used effectively to her purpose. But never in her life had she been accused of a single unselfish act.

Bonnie finished with her hair and lighted a cigarette. She crossed her stockinged legs and thought idly of Wyckoff in the other room. He would be dead at this moment if the case had contained all of the money.

Well, it was only a matter of time and she didn't particularly care as long as she didn't see it happen, since violence made her slightly uncomfortable. It reminded her too much of her own fragility. She was living too close to violence. It might reach out and touch her. People who got in her way should just be made to vanish forever and without fuss.

Too bad about Wyckoff. If he had proven his willingness to ditch his wife for her, she could have lived, with him, an entirely different sort of life, more suitable to her regal tastes.

Bonnie could adapt herself to almost anyone who was able to

supply her with a continuous abundance of luxury. Except in the sense of animal attraction, love was a word without meaning for her.

She had once believed that she was in love with Larry, consumed by the need of him, reduced by the force of his magnetism to a state of slavish adoration—which, translated into basic urge, meant only that he aroused more desire than any other male who had locked eyes with her since her first timid experiment at fourteen.

She had met Larry in Miami. He was dating her roommate at the time. But this was a minor obstacle to a callous conscience and she took him over immediately.

During this period Larry was a Syndicate bookie in charge of a territory. He was not typical of the breed since he had gone to college and had a certain polish, a hard, smooth veneer. For a brief interval he had made an "honest" living at a variety of desk jobs, quietly taking the small bets of office personnel wherever he found himself.

In addition to his arrogant charm and dominant maleness, he seemed to have an inexhaustable supply of expendable cash, and this was enough for Bonnie. If a man had it, she didn't care how he got it. Anyway, in Bonnie, larceny was practically a native instinct.

When a new Miami administration slammed the door in the face of nearly open gambling, Larry was ordered by the Syndicate to take up the richer rewards of southern California.

It was a time of decision for Bonnie. As usual, she thought it all out, calculating profit and loss. She decided against Larry's offer of marriage, then promptly (for the first and last time) followed her emotions and married him anyway. They moved to Los Angeles.

Bonnie had good reason to hesitate before leaping into a kind of frenzied marital bliss. She was the sort whose queenly manner and dress attracted the eye and pocket-book of the big owners and spenders. To these she was a challenge, the vintage champagne of females, much to be desired for play and display. At the very moment of decision, two such loaded specimens were in hot pursuit.

One was the owner of a drugstore chain, a widower who guaranteed living on the most lavish scale. But he was a terrible creep who smoked foul cigars and had a face like a frog. Also, he was sixty and in disgustingly good health. Even Bonnie had her limits.

The other was forty-one, tall dark and sneeringly handsome. He was a light-complected Brazilian with tons of money, all of it bearing the faint aroma of coffee. In public he had beautiful manners. In bed he was savage. He made rape seem rather childish and gentle. His lips promised a fortune in Brazil. His eyes promised unspeakable cruelty and servitude. Did she really want to go to Brazil? And with him?

There were others, but they had wives. So she married Larry. For all her scheming she was too struck with him to do otherwise.

Larry was quick to see her special attraction to rich men as a possible source of giant profit. In his search for a plot he came upon the plan to lure a sucker and hold him for ransom. He discussed it with Bonnie.

She rebelled against the dangers of a life of crime. But on the basis of one big haul which would provide enough loot to fill the rest of her days with splendour and ease, she agreed. It was a simple plan with every chance of success. But since there were then no prospects to suit the exacting requirements of the trap, the idea lay dormant, waiting for Wyckoff.

Meanwhile, Larry had entrenched himself in Los Angeles, taking charge of a segment of the bookie operation for the Syndicate. He was merely treading water, dissatisfied, watching for the jackpot angle to end all angles.

He brought with him from Miami two of his flunkies, Vince Talapka and Brock Swanson. As before, they acted in the dual capacity of runners and enforcers. And though Larry trusted no one, Vince and Brock did precisely as they were told and thus earned a certain dubious loyalty and friendship.

It was the enforcing side of the bookie racket which landed all three of them in San Quentin. There was a man by the name of Max Kromer who owned a bar and B-girl setup downtown. He was an incurable horse bettor who got in too deep. He ran up a tab of twenty-eight thousand and welched. Larry sent Vince and Brock to collect, but they came back with excuses. Kromer had bodyguards with muscles and guns.

"So what?" said Larry. "Do they sleep beside the sonofabitch?"

With Vince and Brock, Larry got into Kromer's bachelor apartment They waited in the dark until after three in the morning. When Kromer entered, they jumped him. They beat him mindless and then Larry produced a cruel knife and carved a lesson on Kromer's face that he would carry to his grave.

The unpredictable happened. The man who lived in the next apartment returned home just behind Kromer. He heard the sounds of horror beyond the door and called the police.

The trio were sent to Quentin, Larry winning the longest term. Bonnie, loyal in her fashion, waited. She kept herself busy hunting rich game. She had Wyckoff cooked—and served him up for Larry soon after his release. Larry enlisted Brock and Vince and Operation Ransom began.

Now Bonnie got up and walked toward the closet, but paused in her stride, listening. Brock's pacing steps had drawn closer, then stopped altogether. Bonnie observed that she had forgotten to lock the door and went quickly to do so. Her hand was reaching out when the knob turned and Brock entered, nearly striking her with the door. He stood gazing at her body with narrowed eyes which were glazed with frenetic desire.

He had thin, blonde hair and blunt, freckled features. He was medium-sized and oddly constructed. He had wide shoulders and massive arms. His chest was rather small and his body tapered sharply to extremely narrow hips so that he appeared top-heavy. He had a loose, rolling walk and there was about him the deceptive innocence of the bear.

"Get out of here, Brock," said Bonnie. "You get the hell out!"

Brock moistened his lips as one does who is a little nervous but still determined. He closed the door and leaned against it, smiling.

"Brock!" She backed away. "Do you know what Larry would do if he caught you?"

"Yeah, sure honey. But he ain't here—see what I mean?"

"You come near me," she warned, "and I'll take this cigarette and jam it right in your eye."

"I'd like to see you try that, honey. I really would, you know."

He moved nearer, sauntering, arms loose at his sides, leering his hunger.

"I've been waitin' a long time for this," he said. "Cruisin' out there, thinkin' about it. Couldn't make up my mind, until just now."

Suddenly he reached out and grabbed the hand with the cigarette, twisted until the butt fell to the floor. He stepped down on it and pulled her in tight against him. She smashed a hand across his face but he hardly noticed.

"Brock, please!" Yet, some perverse part of her was enjoying it.

He had her locked in, muscled arms bulging around her, his hands closing over the back strap of the bra, wrenching, tearing it apart He broke the shoulder straps as if they were ribbons and threw the flimsy garment to the floor. Still holding her, he stood back a bit and marvelled at the sight of her.

She stood proudly now, pretending a look of bored endurance, no longer struggling.

"Go ahead, Brock," she said huskily. "Go right ahead, darling—but of course, I'll tell Larry."

One of his hands disappeared and came back with a broad sharp knife. He held the point just under her eye.

"No, you won't," he said. "Cause if you do, baby, I'll get you alone again, sometime."

She looked down along the blade of the knife and the bright flame of her ego went out in a chill wind of fear.

"I think you would," she said. "I think you'd do it."

The knife vanished and she turned, pressing against him, running her hands over his back.

"But you won't have to, Brock," she gasped. "Because whatever you do to me now—no matter how bad it is—I'll never say a word."

"That's the girl," he said. "I knew we'd get along the minute I laid eyes on you. Don't know why I waited so long."

"Wait, darling. Don't tear. I'll take them—"

She suddenly went rigid. They both froze in a startled tableau, listening.

"A car," she said in a hoarse whisper. "They're back. Go! Hurry! Get out, get out!"

He was gone, almost before the words died. She picked up the torn bra, hid it in a drawer, pulled on another. In seconds she had stepped into slacks and was frantically buttoning a blouse while studying her make-up in the mirror.

She heard the car door shut, then the muted thump of the front door. She wrenched her shoulders back and stepped into the living room, her face sealed by the haughty expression behind which she hid all her secrets.

Larry was alone. He gave her only a quick side-glance, moving toward Brock, now slumped in a chair, yawning as he dropped the newspaper to his lap.

"Hi, Dug," he said. "Where's Vince?"

"Over at the Columbus. I had him staked out in the lobby when I made the call. If there's any action, if the cops move in, he'll spot 'em. How's lover boy behaving?"

"Not a peep. A regular zombie in chains. He don't move, never says a word. Even when he knew we were gettin' ready to finish him, he was a clam. Plenty of guts, I'll say that for 'im."

Larry gave a depreciating little grunt and Bonnie approached, watching him carefully, smiling. His eyes slid over her in the manner of one whose attention is largely inward. But he winked and she almost sighed audibly in relief.

Larry Duggan was three inches over six feet tall, a solid, raw-boned type, broad of shoulder and chest, thick of arm, long of leg. He had wiry reddish-brown hair and sullen brown eyes with a fixed challenging alertness. His high cheekbones were unusually large and protruding, so that his lower face appeared oddly concave. This, together with a dark skin, a high overhang of forehead, gave him a look of latent savagery. There was such a wide spread to his thin-lipped mouth that even when angry he appeared to smile mockingly.

At 38 he was neither ugly nor handsome but a peculiar mixture of both. He had a special magnetism for women like Bonnie who did not care about looks so much as the force of manhood, the dynamic tension of an unrelenting personality. There was also a surface polish to Larry. He spoke softly in a rich, deep voice and could, on occasion, summon the best of manners and comment intelligently on a wide range of subjects, including the arts. This latter was important to Bonnie. She had once been a minor actress and was convinced that she should have been a star, only the present-day slobs who produced plays had obstructed her. They were thick-skinned idiots, crass businessmen who knew nothing of a subtle and sensitive talent.

"Well," she said to Larry, "how did it go with the ransom call? Did you twist him our way, darling?"

He shook his head. "The sonofabitch held out, wouldn't budge. He didn't seem to care when I told him we'd send him Wyckoff in sections if we didn't get the cash tonight. He was cool, no heart—a real wise guy, too."

"Aw, he was prob'ly bluffin'," Brock said.

"No, he wasn't bluffing." Bonnie had taken a chair and now Larry sat on the arm, scratching his chin. "I got a little ball in my head that clicks into a slot when someone is trying to bluff me. This guy sounded like he was sitting there with four aces."

"I wonder who he is," said Bonnie.

"Maybe they sent a cop," said Brock.

"Maybe," Larry answered. "If so, we'll find out. We can handle one cop. Meanwhile we sit tight and play along. We've got no choice."

"Sure we have," said Brock behind a cloud of smoke. "We can blow, just fade away with the hundred grand."

"Now listen," said Larry, getting up and leaning over Brock's chair so that their faces were just inches apart. "There's only one way you're gonna fade out of this deal before it's over, buddy. You wanted in and you got in—for the whole ride. I've had it from you, Brock. For the last time, just shut up and do as you're told. Understand?"

"Sure, Dug," Brock smiled. "Anything you say, kiddo."

But when Larry had turned his back, Bonnie caught Brock's wink of defiance which he sent to her over Larry's shoulder. And she though: *That's his brave little attempt to show me he's not afraid. But he is, I can tell. Let him try to touch me again. Just let him try!*

"What about the DiNardo Girl?" she said.

"I called her place." Larry sat down again on the arm of the chair. "No answer. Can't figure where she is this time of night, Bonnie. We've got to find her—fast I don't know how she did it, but she caught on to something. She couldn't know it all, but she may know part of it. Otherwise, why was she snooping around that parking lot, playing girl detective?" He turned to Brock. "Lying bitch! She was hiding there, she followed us. I tried to talk her into the car. But when it didn't work I had to play it dumb, as if we believed her. I couldn't grab her right there on the steps of the hotel."

"So, what now?" said Brock.

"We'll have old Talbot ring her phone all night." Larry grinned. "And if she doesn't answer, I'll go over and see if she's really out

That one's got to be stopped before she blabs."

"Stopped?" said Bonnie.

"That's right. Stopped!"

"I don't like it," Brock grumbled. "It's gettin' too complicated."

"Shut up," said Larry.

"He's right," Bonnie agreed. "It's becoming pretty damn involved. What about Ingram? Next thing you know we'll be stopping her, too."

"If I say so, we'll stop the whole goddamn town before it's over," Larry snapped. "Now shut up! Both of you, just shut up!"

He crossed rapidly to the phone, lifted the receiver and began to dial.

Bonnie saw that Brock was staring at her. She read his mind. *Why don't we take the hundred grand and beat it together?* he was thinking.

With her eyes she gave him a cool *No Sale.* Yet, she could see the first small cracks in the wall of the plan. And she could hear the soundless little voice that always warned her when trouble was coming.

CHAPTER ELEVEN

'Give me the room number of Mrs. Mildred J. Talbot," said Bryan to the room clerk at the Dupont as Pauline stood by.

The clerk went away, came back.

"Sorry, sir, she checked out two or three hours ago."

"Any forwarding?"

"No, sir. I looked."

"Has her room been cleaned yet?"

"I'm sure it hasn't, sir."

"Well, this lady was visiting Mrs. Talbot earlier and she may have left her cigarette lighter in the room—a gold combination lighter and watch, quite valuable."

"Yes but that's not the point," added Pauline. "It was given to me by—well, it has a sentimental attachment."

"I understand." The clerk smiled. "I'll send a boy up to hunt for it."

"I wonder if we could go along?" Bryan asked. "The lady might have a better idea where she mislaid it."

"Certainly. I'll have a bellhop for you in a minute."

The boy arrived with a key and they followed him across the lobby to an elevator. The car stopped at nine and they went down the hallway to a door. The bellhop opened the door and they went in.

There was a small sitting room, a bedroom and bath. The bed was made and there was little evidence that anyone had used the rooms.

Pauline began a search of the sofa, lifting pillows, then getting down on her knees to peer around the floor beneath. While the bellhop poked around tables and chairs, Bryan wandered into the bathroom and, finding nothing, moved on to the bedroom.

One closet—empty. A night table drawer—empty. A vanity and dresser—empty. A waste basket—containing one brown silk stocking, with a beaut of a run, and a piece of grey paper of the type used to wrap his father's watch. These he tucked in his pocket. After an exploration under the bed, he made a careful examination of the rug. He found two black hairs and these he placed in an envelope before returning to the sitting room.

"Any luck?" he asked cheerfully.

"No, sir," the bellhop answered. "Not yet."

"I must have lost it somewhere else," said Pauline with a little shake of her head to indicate she had found nothing of interest.

Bryan crossed to the desk—underneath, an empty waste basket, on the desk, nothing. The drawer held only the hotel stationery. He searched the rug and, after discovering another strand of black hair which he added to his collection, said, "Better give up, it's not here. Somehow, we'll locate Mrs. Talbot She may have taken the lighter with her."

He gave the bellhop a couple of bucks and told him he wanted to talk with the switchboard operator. The boy guided them to her cubbyhole and departed.

"Do you keep a record of outgoing calls?" he asked the girl.

"Yes, sir. If the calls are fairly recent we would have a record. I make out a slip on every number called."

"And what happens to those slips?"

"They go on to auditing."

"How soon after you write up the slip?"

"When I finish my trick, unless a customer checks out. Then auditing-contacts me for charges. Can I help you with something, sir?"

"I hope so. We're trying to locate Mrs. Mildred J. Talbot She was in Nine-twelve but she checked out awhile ago without leaving a forwarding address. We're friends and we must find her. It's important. We thought perhaps if we had the numbers she called we could trace her. See what I mean?"

"Oh, yes, sir. I understand. But I'm afraid that's a little irregular. Of course, if you wanted to talk with the assistant manager, maybe—"

"We wouldn't have time for red tape," said Bryan. He reached in his pocket and placed a pre-folded ten-dollar bill on the board. "Now be a pal and see what you can do for us."

"Well," said the operator as she palmed the bill, "you do look like very nice people."

She made a rapid search of slips impaled on a spindle, shook her head negatively. "Nothing tonight. I'll have to check the file in auditing. It's only a few steps away. Alice!" she called. "Oh, Alice, will ya take over for a minute?"

Alice relieved her and she disappeared. She was back in a couple of minutes. She handed Bryan a folded piece of paper as Alice departed. "Just two locals," she said. "That's all I could find."

"Thanks," said Bryan with a wink. "You're a big help."

"Don't tell anyone, now," she pleaded.

"Scout's honour," said Bryan, and hurried Pauline out of the hotel.

In an all-night drug-store they sat in a booth over coffee and stared at the slip with its two numbers. "Why, that second number is mine!" said Pauline. "Great And what about the other?"

"It doesn't mean a thing to me."

"Okay," said Bryan. "Just sit tight. I'm going over to that booth and dial this, see who answers."

"No," said Pauline. "Suppose it turned out to be that man you talked to earlier about the ransom? He might recognize your voice."

"I don't expect to have that kind of luck. She wouldn't be stupid' enough to call the hide-out from a hotel. I'm sure of that. Just the same, maybe *you'd* better try it. Ask who's speaking, then play wrong number." He gave her a dime and she went off to the booth. She returned quickly, shaking her head.

"No answer. What next? Could information give you the address of that number?"

"They won't do it. I tried that once. We'll keep ringing. If we don't have any luck; then we'll get a phone book and go to work together, each taking half. We won't check for the whole number, just the last two digits. That way we can scan quickly. C'mon, I'll take you home. We'll dial again from your place."

CHAPTER TWELVE

Pauline's apartment was Just off the Venetian Causeway, a few blocks from the beach. Bryan had a hunch they were being followed when the taxi made the second turn after leaving the Causeway and the lights of the car were still behind. He said nothing to Pauline but watched as he paid the fare. A white Cadillac slid past. A man and a woman were in it, and they both seemed oblivious to Bryan's stare. The car vanished around a corner, but Bryan was not convinced.

They climbed an outside stairway to the second landing and followed a breezeway to a door. Pauline worked her key and they went in.

It was a large rectangle of living room done predominantly in black and white with colour accents and blonde mahogany tables in relief. The furnishings displayed good taste at considerable expense.

"Nice," said Bryan politely. "Very impressive." He moved about the room, surveying it absently, his mind far from such low-key interests as decor.

She smiled her appreciation. "A drink? I have Scotch and bourbon, or there's some—"

"Fine, fine. Anything at all with a boost."

She lighted lamps, cut the overhead glare and went off to another room, presumably the kitchen. He heard the clink of glasses, the slam of a refrigerator door as he strode to a window and peered out to the street.

For a few moments there was nothing, then he saw the white Cadillac returning, gliding slowly past. He recognized the car as a current model, like one his mother had for her personal use.

Quickly he doused the lights and hurried back to the window. The Cadillac wheeled on for half a block, turned in a driveway, backed and manoeuvred into a place at the kerb. The headlights winked out.

He heard Pauline enter behind him.

"What happened?" she said. "Did we blow a fuse or do you see better in the dark?" She tried to sound gay but her voice was tremulous.

"Is there another way out?" he asked, still watching. "A back door?"

"No, just the front." She came to stand by his side, a glass in each hand.

He took one of the glasses from her and drank deeply, not caring that it was straight bourbon on the rocks.

"What do you see, Bryan? What do you see?"

"Man and woman in a white Cadillac. They followed our taxi."

"You didn't tell me!" she gasped.

"I wasn't sure. Car's parked down about half a block on the left and facing this way."

She followed his gaze. "It's so dark," she said. "I can just about—yes, I see it! You're positive?"

"Positiva."

"Then, what does it mean?"

"It means the couple in that car could be the key. If I could grab him … I'm going down, Pauline."

"No! No, it would be dangerous. Besides, if they're watching, they'd see you. With the lights out here, they must already suspect something."

He gulped his drink and put down the glass. "I want a look from your bedroom. But first we'll draw the blinds and turn on a light."

This done, he followed her along a hallway to an open door. She reached for the light switch but he grabbed her wrist and went to the window and opened it. He looked down upon an alley behind the building.

"It's not too far," he said. "Not if I hang from the sill." He worked the slide of the automatic, arming it, returning it to his pocket. He prepared to climb out but she caught his hand and squeezed.

"Be careful," she said. "Oh, do be careful!"

Her soft voice in the darkness was touched with such woeful concern that he turned suddenly, enfolding her in his arms. She met his kiss hungrily, pouring into her response a mixture of need and passion, a reluctance to let him go. All this was communicated with a moist, searching mouth which trembled over his.

He broke away gently, climbed onto the sill, reversed his body and hung downward. He fell relaxed, letting his knees absorb the shock. He recovered, got the gun in his fist and began to step lightly toward the side street, intending to circle and come up behind the Cadillac. He had just reached the edge of the building when he heard the starting pulse of a big motor, saw the yellow-white of headlights.

He sprinted around the corner to the street fronting the buildings, thinking that some instinct had warned the guy and he must not let him get away.

He raced across the street diagonally as the car moved slowly toward him. He paused near the kerb, straight-arming his gun at the windshield, ordering a stop with his left palm raised.

Instantly there was the sound of acceleration and the lights rushed upon him. He danced sideways over the kerb, the car following with a thump of tyre on cement. The front fender grazed his thigh, hurling him to the ground. The car swerved and regained the street, howled around a corner—gone.

He picked himself up, brushing grass and dirt from his clothes, marvelling that he was uninjured. He had lost the gun but soon found it on the edge of the walk where it had slid from his hand. Rubbing his thigh, he went slowly back to the apartment.

"I saw it all," said Pauline breathlessly, "from the window. I—I thought he was going to kill you."

"Close," said Bryan. "Too close. I was a damn fool, because when I had a chance to shoot, I didn't. But hell, you can't blast away at a guy just because he was parked with a girl in a car and seemed to be watching. It could have been a coincidence. But then, when I knew it wasn't, it was too late." He finally got a cigarette going with an unsteady hand, leaned against the door and sighed.

"Are you all right, Bryan? You weren't hurt?" She came toward him in the dim glow from a single lamp, her face shadowed with anxiety.

"I've been knocked around before, much worse." He grinned.

She reached up and smoothed his hair. "Well, at least they're gone. You got rid of them."

"For a while.

"I may have a bonus, but I think it was you who was being watched, Pauline. They'll be back, much more cautious next time—or they'll send someone else."

"Then I can't stay here alone. I wouldn't dare."

"Must you stay here—alone?"

Her eyes slid away from his face. "Do you want me to call that number again?"

"Good idea. Give it a whirl."

He handed her the slip and she went to the phone, dialled. After a time she cradled the receiver. "Still no answer."

"Then we've got work to do. We'll need a telephone book and a couple of drinks." She brightened. "Coming up," she said.

For a while they sat side by side on the sofa, each taking half the book, sipping bourbon as they scanned.

"Got it!" said Pauline, who had the first half. "Norma DiNardo. 326½ Archway Drive."

"Let me see that!" He took the book from her. "No doubt about it, that's our baby. You want an educated guess?"

"I'm way ahead of you, Bryan. You're going to tell me that Norma DiNardo is probably the other girl, the second phony agent."

"Right. And with luck, we'll catch up with her tomorrow. I'm damn well not going to go wandering around her place tonight. Someone might call the cops. I'm not ready for cops, not yet."

Pauline found a pencil and wrote down the address. "What now?" she said. "You're still such a stranger to me. Couldn't you take even fifteen minutes out to tell me something about yourself?"

He sighed. "Sure. You've earned the right to be curious. In fifteen minutes I could give you a rough outline. The rest would kill fifteen days."

"Just the outline, then. Please."

He told her the fundamentals of his existence and she asked appropriate questions. Then he said, "Well, I suppose we'll function better with a little sleep. I'll take the couch."

She patted his cheek, gave him a quick kiss. "You're a very nice guy, know that?"

"Huh! Wait'll you get to know me better, Pauline. Give me a chance."

"Maybe I will," she said. "Maybe I will."

CHAPTER THIRTEEN

He lay on the sofa in the dark. He had not been able to sleep and was lying on his back, smoking. The gun was near him on the coffee table.

He heard Pauline come out of the bathroom. A finger of light fell across the carpet, then vanished.

"You, too?" he called.

In a moment there was the pad of her feet and her shadow drifted beside him, wrapped in a negligee. "Me, too," she murmured. "Now go to sleep."

"You could help."

"Oh no, I couldn't."

"Yes, you could. Rub my fevered brow."

She hovered there for a moment uncertainly. "Scrunch over, then," she said.

He moved, and she sat down and began to rub his head. They were silent.

But in a minute she said, "Don't you really care what happens to your father?"

"I'd rather not talk about it now."

"Obviously you do care or you wouldn't risk so much to help him."

"Wouldn't I?"

"No."

"Then you have your answer, don't you?"

"I want to hear you say it."

"That's silly."

"No, it isn't. Because I couldn't understand a man who had no love for his father."

"Love has to be earned. And don't give me platitudes."

"But when someone's in trouble in your own family, doesn't your heart reach out to him?"

For a long moment he was unable to answer. "Don't make it difficult for me, Pauline."

"There!" she said. "That catch in your voice—it gave you away."

"All right, all right," he said gruffly. "Some big part of me cares a hell of a lot. But I can't afford to admit it while this job has to be done. Don't you see?"

"Yes, I see very well." And then she leaned down and kissed him, softly at first, then violently.

"Oh, I knew this would happen, I knew it!" she moaned. Her lips sought his and they began to kiss, silently, passionately.

He moved his arms under her and stood up, lifting her in his arms. He carried her to the bed and laid her down gently. She reached her arms out and drew him down to her.

It was almost dawn when she said, "Now I can sleep, darling. Now I could sleep for an age."

But he heard her as from a great distance, for he was already floating downward into a dark, delicious void.

In the morning they found 326½ Archway Drive in a surprisingly exclusive residential area. The address became understandable when they discovered that it designated a small guest house behind an imposing but ancient mansion. The big house was sealed by storm shutters. Evidently the owner had been absent for many months and had allowed the grounds to deteriorate. Grass and shrubs grew in a wild tangle, a tall surrounding hedge of hibiscus mushroomed out of control, long in need of trimming.

Bryan steered Pauline's Chewy up the drive to a garage. Here they parked and walked around back to the guest house, a looking clapboard structure in need of new paint. The shades were drawn. There was no bell button. Bryan knocked, sharply and continuously, without success.

"What do you think?" said Pauline, her drawn face revealing dismay. "Could something have happened to her?"

"Just about everything, under the circumstances. Still, I'd hate to break in."

"Why don't we leave a note?" Pauline suggested. "With my name and telephone number. Ask her to call me the minute she comes in and say it's urgent. I'll put C.I.A. next to my name. If she doesn't know what that means it won't hurt. And if she does—"

"Okay. Good idea. Curiosity alone should compel her to phone. If she doesn't call before night, I'll force a window and have a look."

Pauline wrote the note and slipped it under the door.

"Now back to my place to wait," she said. "Unless you can think of a better way to use the time."

Once the grin got started, Bryan couldn't contain its progress across his face.

"I only meant," she added hastily, "that I could sit by the phone while you were free to go wherever you might need to."

"Aw, I'm disappointed. I thought you meant something entirely different."

"Darling, when this nightmare is over, I *will* mean something entirely different. You know, that's only the second time I've ever seen you really smile."

"Is it? Well, stick around. Maybe in a couple of days I might smile again. I've kicked the habit for the time being."

She squeezed his hand. "I know, Bryan. I know. Shall we drive on to my place? Or have you another clue you could follow?"

"No, we'll go to your apartment and mull over what we've got Unless this Norma DiNardo calls, I don't think there's much I can do until after I talk to my father at seven."

She nodded solemnly.

"But if they don't put him on the line tonight, I'm going to light a fire under the police, the FBI and the newspapers. Then you'll see the biggest goddamn manhunt since the Lindbergh case."

CHAPTER FOURTEEN

It was early afternoon. They were at Pauline's apartment and Bryan was pacing her living room. He paused, stared at the phone and said, "Ring, damn you, ring!" Then he went pacing, stopped and turned to Pauline.

She sat in a chair, examining a brown silk stocking.

"Well?" he said.

She shook her head. "It's a good grade, all right, but a very common brand. You'd find it in almost any store where stockings are sold. The size would be about right for Talbot But you could check every shop in town and it would be useless because they don't take names and addresses on a cash sale. Now, if she had a charge account somewhere …"

"No good," said Bryan. "I know damn well that Talbot isn't her right name. It couldn't be. Otherwise, she could be traced. She'd figure that out She sounds like a smart cookie. So what does that leave us? A piece of grey wrapping paper you could get in any drugstore, and this."

He passed her the envelope containing the three strands of long black hair.

She opened the envelope and removed the strands. "Where did you find these?"

"Same place. Two on the rug by the vanity in Talbot's bedroom, one in the sitting room, also on the rug."

"These must belong to some gal who had the room before Talbot," Pauline said.

"Must they? Those rooms get a pretty good cleaning."

"Well, suppose she had a visitor?"

"It's possible. But I don't picture a visitor sitting at her vanity. I don't picture a visitor combing her hair all over the place."

"What are you trying to say, Bryan?"

"That those hairs could belong to Talbot."

"But how could they? Talbot has blonde hair streaked with grey."

"So?"

They stared at each other.

"I'm reading you," said Pauline. "You think she dyed her hair or treated it in some way."

"Yes. Or she used a wig. Then she could have had a disguise which made her look years older, just adding a touch here and there."

Pauline nodded decisively. "That could be it! I had the feeling all along that her face was a little too smooth-skinned for her age. And her hands—a woman's hands usually show her age. Talbot's hands didn't have a wrinkle. I remember thinking that she must take very good care of herself, but I never suspected."

"Okay. So she wore a disguise—that still doesn't help much."

"It might," said Pauline. "I could do a sketch of her from memory. I've done a lot of retouching and I used to make a few sketches of people from photographs. If I do say so, they weren't bad. I'll use pastels and give Talbot black hair. Then maybe we'll begin to get some idea of what she really looks like."

"How long will it take?"

"Twenty minutes to an hour, depending on my recall."

"Go ahead, then. Anything beats wasting time."

Pauline left the room and returned with a drawing board, a box of pastels, pencil and paper. She worked for half an hour, refusing to allow Bryan a look until she was finished.

"Now!" she said. "This is about the way Talbot looked as I remember her. Come and see, then I'll fix the hair."

Bryan leaned over the board, seeing the head-and-shoulders pastel of a distinguished-looking woman with grey-blonde hair and harlequin glasses. The hair was arranged in a chignon which added severity to the features.

"Not a bad-looking dame," he said. "Mid-forties and well preserved, I'd guess. What sort of figure did she have?"

"Good. In fact, I'd call it statuesque. She was quite—uh—chesty."

"Uh-huh. All right, now let's see the hair in black."

Pauline selected a black stick from the box and quickly darkened the hair. Bryan stood back.

"Ahh," he said. "See the difference? She lost at least ten years." He studied the portrait with the unfounded conviction that they were moving toward some oblique revelation. "Suppose we took the hair down, Pauline. Could you do that?"

"Sure. What style would you like?"

"Style? I don't know a damn thing about style. Make it simple."

"Okay. We'll try a pageboy."

She erased the knot from the hair, drew it down to the shoulders, introduced bangs.

"Wow! Another five years," said Bryan.

"A good five years. And she's rather beautiful, don't you think?"

Bryan didn't answer. The pastel had caught him in a strange fascination, oddly disturbing.

"Lose the glasses," he said. "They're bound to be phony."

She gazed up at him quizzically, then removed the glasses with a special eraser.

"A girl in her late twenties," he murmured. "Striking, positively striking. Now, do something with her mouth. You've made it too thin and proper. Give me full sexy lips."

Again she looked up at him, frowning, perplexed. She went to work.

"That's it, Pauline. Now you've almost got it. But I don't like the nose—hump it slightly at the bridge and thicken it around the nostrils."

She put down the stick and plucked her cigarette from a tray. She stared at him intently. "Bryan, is this your conception—or mine?"

"Talk later. Right now, do as I say," he snapped, not taking his eyes from the portrait.

With a shrug, Pauline made the adjustments to the nose altering it as he stood by, giving direction.

He leaned back, observing the face with satisfaction.

"That's close enough," he said. "Isn't that more like her nose? And her mouth?"

She gave the features a squinting attention. "Yes—much more precise." She turned to look at him with wonder. "Where did you meet her, Bryan?"

He crossed the room and fell into a chair, lighting a cigarette, feeling spent.

"I met her in New York. It must be five—no, six months ago. Her real name is Bonnie—Bonnie Duggan. She was an actress—at least, she was trying to be and couldn't make the big time. She had one or two fair parts in seedy off-Broadway houses. I was travelling with the bunch like her who were—well, in the vestibule of the theatre, not really in, not really out. I've always been sympathetic with those sad, driven people who couldn't quite shove over the line.

"Anyway, I met Bonnie at a hectic little party to celebrate the success of an actress who finally did get a decent part in a Broadway comedy scheduled to open last fall. It was typical of Bonnie that she was violently jealous, covering her true emotions with torrents of praise—though I must admit I didn't see it then. She was just another gal on fire. But she had a queenly charm and the most marvellous equipment for—uh—the kind of play you'll never see on Broadway. She could freeze you out or she could turn on a sneaky sex magnetism that would electrify all of Times Square.

"I think she had an idea that I could do something for her because I had been falsely accused of having wealth and in
So she fell on me like a ton of aphrodisiacs and the next thing you know we were in a taxi on the way to my apartment. That's how it got started."

"This is fantastic!" said Pauline. "There just has to be a connection that leads to your father."

"Of course. I can see that now."

"Did you ever introduce her to him?"

"As I told you, I haven't laid eyes on my Old Man in years."

"But you knew this Bonnie very well?"

"I thought so. Evidently I didn't know her at all."

How well he had known Bonnie was not a tale for Pauline—a tale of sensual involvement that had reached ecstatic heights and degrading depths—because though he had grown to despise Bonnie he had been unable to shake the physical need of her.

"Please go on," said Pauline. "I'm fascinated. Tell me the whole thing."

"No—just the essentials, Pauline. It was nothing but a grubby little affair that only appeared to have some basis for continuing more than the few weeks it lasted. I talked myself into thinking we shared an interest in the theatre and writing, that we both had a realistic view of living. But Bonnie was an egomaniac who fell in love with herself at age two and never got over it.

"She pretended an enormous sympathy with my personal problems, so I told her about my fight with the Old Man. It seemed like the big unburdening then, but now I realize that she was pumping me from the time she found out two things—one, that I had no more than an income from a trust fund because my father had disowned me; two, that he had one great weakness: he was a skirt-chaser."

"You mean," said Pauline, "she was planning to have your father kidnapped even then?"

"No. I don't think so, not then. I figure she schemed to meet him and milk him. The kidnap plan probably came later when she did meet him and found him not so easy to con. For all his money, he's pretty close with a buck."

"What else do you know about her? Did she have any underworld friends?"

"Not that she ever mentioned—not that I ever saw, either. According to what she told me, she had once lived in Miami for a short time, but she came up to New York from Washington. She had some kind of secretarial job with a branch of the government. She was vague about it, said she worked with classified material. Could have been C.I.A., for all I know. She was in little theatre, too, caught the bug. That's why she quit and came to New York. And—let's see—she was married but separated. Her husband lived in San Francisco, said she would get a divorce if she ever had a real excuse. And that's it. The rest is incidental."

"But how did it end? Did you just drift apart?"

"Oh, no. We had a fight and I didn't see her for a few days. Then one evening I went over to her apartment and she had moved—just gone—no one knew where. And after a while I decided it was for the best and stopped trying to find her."

"Somehow she met your father," mused Pauline. "And after that she certainly didn't want to have anything more to do with you."

"Naturally not-And meeting my Old Man would be no problem for a girl with her magnetism—and imagination. She knew some of his habits. She knew where to go so that she could make a seemingly accidental contact with him. It might have taken her a week or two, but she was determined and clever. Nothing to it, because the minute she got him into conversation, she had him. He'd do the rest. You wave the red cape at the bull and the game is on."

"How strange and evil," said Pauline. "And yet, how marvellous, because now you've got the solution."

"Have I? You make it sound simple. What do I really have to work with? That Bonnie Duggan is involved in the kidnapping of my father, that she probably got help from some real pros, that she once lived in Miami and knows the town. It's a big town containing over a million people and unlimited places to hide. Now all I've got to do is find her. Tell me how?"

Pauline smiled. "We could start with the phone book."

"I'm laughing, but go ahead."

She reached for the book, thumbed quickly and shook her head. "Not under Bonnie or Bonita. Did she ever use her married name?"

"No. But let's see—she referred to her husband as Larry."

Pauline looked again, then said, "Nope, not under Larry or Lawrence Duggan, either."

Bryan said, "If they're holding him in a place where there's a phone, it won't be listed under any name we ever heard of. Forget it." He got up and went to the door. "I'm going to check the auto licence bureau, the utility companies, department stores, anyplace where there might be a record of some transaction requiring Bonnie's name and address."

"Couldn't you do some of that by phone, Bryan?"

"Maybe. But let's keep your line open for a call from Norma DiNardo. She might have something important we can use."

"Why don't you take my car?"

"Mind?"

"Not at all." She tossed him the keys.

"Pauline, you mustn't feel under any obligation to me. You were just another victim in this filthy mess. You ought to pull out and hide somewhere until it's over. I wish you would, for your own safety."

"I couldn't do that," she said. "I wouldn't be able to live with myself. And if you don't understand that, I can't explain."

He came and kissed her tenderly.

"You get to know people best in a crisis," he said. "That's

when the phonies duck fast I'm beginning to know you very well, Pauline. I haven't needed anyone in such a long while. It's good to need someone."

"Oh, Bryan, Bryan. I think you've always been full of needing, but you were afraid to admit it I've been hurt too, but I'm not hiding from myself. I'm still hungry for love."

"And I vote you the gal most likely to get it," he said with pretended lightness. "Now take this."

He offered her the automatic and she took it reluctantly. He showed her how to use it.

"Keep the door locked, Pauline, and the windows. Don't open the door for anyone but me. If some character tries to break in, shoot him! Don't plead, don't threaten, just aim and pull the trigger."

He kissed her again and went out.

CHAPTER FIFTEEN

Norma DiNardo returned home at twenty minutes after five that afternoon. Light was seeping from the sky as she rode in the cab. And as she approached the guesthouse behind the old mansion, the final curtain of darkness fell with the swiftness of winter.

Norma searched the mailbox and because she found nothing, a small extra weight was added to a depression which had been growing upon her all the way home. She had spent the night with Herm Frawley, a salesman from the Sunkool Awning Company.

Herm was a real fun guy, always ready for a kick at any hour, especially if the kick involved the sort of free love which was not complicated by the necessity of dinner and drinks. He had been more than willing to interrupt his sleep to entertain Norma in her loneliness. In fact, he took the following day off and they had lounged around his apartment. He had allowed Norma to cook his meals between frenzied manoeuvers in the bedroom.

Norma did not mind cooking for Herm; it gave her a sense of domesticity. She enjoyed the sex and was grateful for companionship. But as usual, she went to Herm with the hopeful expectation that this time he would offer at least a fragment of that affection for which she yearned. On the contrary, Herm was emotionally cool in all rooms but the bedroom; even there, his endearments were terse, clinical and often obscene.

Thus Norma left him with the feeling that she had merely been used. She did not even draw close enough to Herm to trust him with the knowledge of her secret employment, an adventure which she had been bursting to confide to him. She had simply paid the usual price that all men demand for a few hours of their stupid company. And afterwards she became more wretched than if she had been sealed in that closet of her mind where she created dream pictures of people who never failed her.

Herm did not offer to take her home on the grounds that he had another date within the hour so there wouldn't be time. In the taxi, Norma made herself a solemn promise: henceforth she would not see Herm Frawley again and her entire loyalty would go to her job. But as she unlocked her door, she realized that she was not really sure of her new job. Whatever her reasons, Mrs. Talbot had lied to her, and Norma wasn't going to forgive that unless she was given a most convincing reason for this deceit.

Norma flipped the light switch and closed the door, locking it. Because she was in such a state of distraction, she did not see the note by her feet. She went immediately to her bedroom and, after removing her dress and shoes, turned out the lamp and lay down in her slip.

For a minute her mind was vacant; there was only the ache of her weariness. Then slowly, the stony, unresponsive image of Herm came to her. How she had debased herself by running to him in the middle of the night, and how dreary was the sameness of all her relations with men. Overwhelmed with self-pity, she turned her head into the pillow and began to cry softly.

Her mood changed abruptly and she was consumed with anger. They'd see who'd use who from now on. Any man who took her out hereafter was going to get teased silly. And he was going to be made to buy and buy, pay and pay before she gave in, while she would be choking in his face to keep from laughing. And then— "Shove off, sonny boy, thanks for the ride," and on to the next sucker. And when a really ripe one came along with gallons of gold, she'd sweet talk and sweet love him right into her trap and marry him. Damn right!

She got up and crossed to her bureau, reaching into her purse for a cigarette. At that moment she heard an arrogant tapping at her door. At first she decided it might be Wilma Kopeck, a child's nurse who lived up the block and sometimes dropped in unexpectedly. But the knocking had a masculine sound. It was just the way Herm used to beat on her door, as if it were a foot thick and she was deaf.

Herm! Maybe he had changed his mind and broken his date and come to her with an apology. *Oh, Herm!* she thought. If *you just say one little kind thing to me, how I'll melt!*

She pulled on a robe and ran in her stocking feet to the door. She twisted the bolt and flung it open.

She was really startled—so much so that she nearly closed the door in his face. But the man in the blue suit, smiling without really smiling at all, stepped in. It was he who closed the door—and locked it! Frightened, she backed away from him, pulling her robe tighter about her.

"Don't be frightened, Norma," he said in the most soothing voice. "I just wanted to be sure we wouldn't be disturbed because I have some top secret business to discuss with you—that's why I locked the door. You see?"

She nodded but was unable to speak.

He glanced around the room. "Ahhh, that's good. You've drawn the shades. That's thoughtful. That's careful—the mark of a good agent, Norma." His eyes dropped and he bent to scoop up a folded piece of white paper. "And what's this, Norma?"

Norma found her voice. "I—I don't know," she said.

"Well, logically we should open it and see, isn't that right?" He unfolded the paper and read, his face expressionless.

He was wearing thin white gloves! They looked transparent. "Where did you get this, Norma?"

"I—I don't even know what it is. I just came home. I guess it's a note. I must have missed it. Let me have it please." She extended her hand.

He seemed not to hear her. He was such an odd man with his over-polite manner, his queerly attractive face, his deep-set eyes, burning like candles flickering from the mouths of dark caves.

"Who are you?" she said. "Excuse me, but I never really knew." *What a silly way for me to talk and act,* she thought, *grovelling like this.* Yet, without effort, without the smallest threat, his presence demanded servility.

"My code name is Larry," he said with a thin-lipped smile. "That's all you need to know for now. I work with Mrs. Talbot to insure the safety of our female agents. Safety—that's the important factor, don't you think?"

"Oh, yes," she said. "Safety first." The very word gave her a sense of relief. She sighed. "You'll have to excuse the way I'm dressed."

"Don't apologize. I should have called." He peered around again. "I don't see a phone."

"It's in the bedroom … Larry."

"I see. Will you show me please, Norma?"

She hesitated, then gestured. "It's that way."

"After, you, Norma." He bowed slightly.

She led him into the bedroom. Immediately he shut the door. And when she couldn't help the tiny recoil of surprise he said, "It's a private call."

"Shall I leave, then?"

"Oh, no. It's not private to you." He sat down on the bed and lifted the receiver. "Sit near me, Norma. I might want you to listen. We'll see."

She sat gingerly, a couple of feet removed. He glanced at her white slip and dialled. After a few moments in which his face was inscrutable, he hung up.

"Nothing," he said. "Too bad."

But Norma thought she heard a female voice.

"On the other hand," he continued, removing his gloves, "maybe there's something wrong with the phone. It had a very dead sound. I'll tell you, Norma, we'll make a new connection to the terminal. First we'll cut the wire and clean the ends."

Everything he said, so gravely put, had a reasonable sound to it yet contained a false note of evil which twisted a knot of uneasiness inside her, tighter and tighter. And still she felt numb and ineffectual, powerless to rebuke him.

She watched him produce the knife with the same casualness of movement with which all his actions were performed. And then he pressed a button, causing an astonishingly long, slim blade to appear.

Norma heard the scream, but it was only in her head. She felt panic rising in her, fear gripped her. *I'm being silly,* she thought, *especially since Larry is only bending the phone cord and cutting it in two.* But then, instead of repairing the wire, he simply tossed the loose ends contemptuously to the floor. And that was when she shrank back from him and began to rise. But with a darting thrust of his hand, he caught her wrist.

"Going some place, Norma?"

"What—what is it you want?"

He held the knife toward her face. "Why did you follow us to the parking lot, Norma?"

"I—why, I didn't. I never did any such thing."

"Norma. The next time you lie, I'm going to sink this knife into your arm. Do you believe me, Norma?"

She stared into his eyes and believed him instantly.

"Why, Norma?"

"I—I just wanted to see where you were going."

"Don't tell me what's obvious, Norma." He slapped her face brutally. "Give me the real reason."

"I wanted—" She began to sob. "I wanted to know where you were taking—taking all that money in the suitcase."

"That's better. And how did you know there was money in the suitcase?"

"I—I—"

"C'mon, c'mon!"

"I saw it—when Mrs. Talbot opened the case in her bedroom. I was watching. The door was—it was open a bit."

"Ahhh. Fine, fine. That's the truth. And the money made you suspicious?"

"Yes." She wiped her eyes. He sounded less angry, really quite friendly.

"What did you suspect? The truth now."

"I don't know exactly. That it was some kind of pay-off for—I really don't know. I just got carried away. I'm sorry."

"You're sorry?"

"Yes."

"Well, that's good. That's very good. But not good enough, Norma."

"What do you mean?"

"It's not safe to have you running around loose with that kind of information."

"Oh, I would never, never tell." She could feel the clammy moisture of sweat between her thighs.

"I can't take the chance, Norma."

"Please, Larry, please! What does that mean?"

"It means I'm going to kill you, Norma."

"No!" She began to tremble violently. "No, no! I'll do any-thing—anything!"

His smile, in the cavity of his face, was polite, almost apologetic. But his hand tightened on her wrist, and the long knife was poised at her throat with cool surgical gleaming.

"I'll—I'll even give myself to you." He drew the knife back.
"You will?"

"Yes. Oh, yes, I will—gladly! You'll see. You'll see, Larry."

The knife descended, resting in his lap.

"Show me, Norma. And don't move toward that door. You'd never make it." He released her wrist.

She did a slow, graceful pivot, and looking down upon him, forced her lips into a terrible smile.

His head nodded approval and the knife blade retreated into the handle with a click.

"You're rather homely, Norma, and not very bright. But you've got a sensational figure, really sensational. Come here, Norma."

She advanced timidly, the smile still petrified upon her face.

"Don't be afraid, Norma," he soothed. "Don't be afraid, sweetheart."

She collapsed against him, her nervous fingers stroking his massive shoulders.

"Don't hurt me, Larry," she whimpered. "Oh, please don't hurt me. You'll never be sorry."

"Poor scared little rabbit," he murmured, kissing her neck. "Now lie on the bed and try to be patient sweet rabbit."

"Oh, Larry," she moaned. "Larry, Larry. Be my lover. Take care of me and be my lover, always, always."

"Your lover, sweet rabbit," he repeated from a hollow distance. "Always, always."

And then with a volcanic shudder, he sighed and was still.

She looked into his face.

The eyes were cooling, the face closing like a door in a sudden shift of wind.

There was the stretching of his arm, the groping of his hand—felt, rather than seen for her eyes were still fastened to his. Then she heard the whisper of metal, the click.

She saw the blade for only an instant, just the wink of steel descending above her chest. As in a stark dream, there seemed more the impression than the reality of a deep searing pain.

And she heard Larry say, from a vast distance, fadingly, "Too bad, little rabbit. Too bad."

CHAPTER SIXTEEN

At ten to seven, Bryan Wyckoff entered his hotel room at the Columbus. He pulled off his jacket, loosened his tie and sat heavily in a chair by the phone. He had talked to Pauline a couple of hours ago and it came to him that he should ring her again.

He grabbed for the receiver, then dropped his hand. Better not chance it. If, by some freak the ransom call was early and the line was busy, the kidnappers might run back to their hole, especially since they would have his father under guard at some booth and the added risk might already be squeezing them close to panic.

The way it was going now, Bryan was discouraged. No one by the name of Bonnie Duggan or Mrs. Larry Duggan held a Florida driver's license. He had no luck at the auto registration bureau or any of the department stores, either. Utility companies, banks, credit bureau—no sale. Phone calls to New York, Washington and the State capital of Tallahassee had uncovered nothing. And according to the long distance operator, there was no Larry Duggan listed in the San Francisco directory. Bryan had thought he might get a clue to Bonnie if he could locate her estranged husband, but it was just another waste of time.

It was all depressingly negative, and only twenty-four hours of time remained. Adding to his burden, the evening paper had carried a story about an eleven-year-old boy who had been kidnapped in Denver. By radio and television the parents had offered to pay double the two hundred thousand demanded in the ransom note—a declaration of terms which did not include the method and place of delivery. They received no answer. Then the boy's strangled, half-buried body had been found in a wood.

Death—the death of his father. It must not happen, even though their differences could not be bridged by a span as far-reaching as the Golden Gate. Yes, Pauline was right. No matter what the surface friction, there was a subconscious bond, an inexorable unity of family in times of deep stress. Yet *he* was right, too, in holding tight, through memory and habit, to the objective view. He knew his whole scheme of rescue depended on cool detachment and consummate skill.

On hotel stationery Bryan began to pen an orderly arrangement of the known facts, counterbalancing them with the unknown, forming conclusions. He did this primarily to discipline his mind away from a growing tension, pushed by the first involuntary leak of his emotions. He had paused to light a cigarette when the phone sounded and he dropped cigarette and lighter to the floor, snatching the receiver.

"Yes?"

"Wyckoff? Bryan Wyckoff?"

He was startled by the unexpected use of his name, spoken by this deep, soft voice with its sullen and disdainful calm.

"This is Brown," he answered.

"Come off it, buddy. We've got you labelled and in the can."

"Okay, I'm Bryan Wyckoff. So what?"

"So it's your Old Man and we'll play by our rules from here to home base, wise guy."

"You think so? Try me."

"I'm ready. You don't get to talk to him and you have the cash set by eleven in the morning. How's that, Wyckoff?"

"No good. I talk to him in ten seconds or I hang up and you don't get the cash at all."

"Don't con me. I don't bluff, Buster."

"Four seconds. You've still got six."

"You snap this connection and you've just shot your Old Man, Wyckoff—right through the head."

"Two seconds. One. Gone!"

He hung up. With a shaking hand, he picked up the lighter and cigarette, brought them together. He sucked in deeply, exhaled a long plume, and the phone rang.

"Just testing, Wyckoff, but don't pull anything clever like a cross. Have the cash by seven tomorrow night and you'll come out on top with a live daddy. You signal cop and we'll blow his brains out Now that one I mean! Here's your Old Man. You got thirty seconds."

There was whispering, the sound of fumbling in a booth, the

hollow clink of the receiver brushing against the coin box.

"Bryan?"

"You all right, Dad?"

"Well enough. What's holding this up. Where's Van? You bail me out and fast, hear?"

"If you want Van, I'll send for him. Meantime, I'll bail you out when I'm goddamn sure I won't get a six hundred thousand dollar corpse. Understand?"

"I understand a lot better than you do, boy. There's just one way out of this and that's the hard way. So give these killers their six hundred thousand and—"

There was a low moan, quickly muffled.

"Tomorrow night at seven. Wyckoff—five hundred grand. We'll send a messenger to your room, a dope who won't know the score. Be ready—or else!"

"Now, listen, you sonofabitch. I won't—"

But they had clicked off, and Bryan was cold certain they had clicked off for good.

He couldn't understand how they learned who he was, unless Bonnie had been watching from some vantage point and had seen him.

He sat for several minutes, analyzing what his father had said. A phrase like "bail me out" did not normally belong in his father's vocabulary. It was legal terminology, insinuating the law—a possible clue. "I understand a lot better than you do," another possible hint. And that crack about one way out, the hard way—for his father, money would be the easier way. And of course the best and most reliable clue was his reference to the kidnappers as "killers".

Adding it up, Bryan decided his father was trying to tell him they would kill him, so get the cops—fast.

For nearly a half-hour he paced, arguing the pros and cons of calling in the police. It was a brutal problem. He couldn't seem to come to a decision.

Finally, he picked up the phone and called his mother.

CHAPTER SEVENTEEN

It was shortly after seven-thirty and Pauline was nervous. She sat in a chair by the window, chain-smoking, attempting to read a magazine. Not much over an hour ago she had answered the phone, thinking it was Bryan. There had positively been someone on the line but that someone, after listening a few seconds to her voice, had hung up.

This happened two or three times before in her life and, particularly since she lived alone, it had frightened her. You met some character in one of those bored periods between the steadies and you went out with him on the feeble hope that he might surprise you. And he did. But it was the wrong kind of surprise. He spent maybe ten bucks for a few drinks and he thought this bought him the right to go beddy-bye four hours from the first time he brought his dubious charms to your door. And when you gave him a polite brush, there was a messy struggle, but you got rid of him.

A couple of days later the phone would ring and perhaps you would hear a kind of laboured breathing, but never a voice. And you would wonder if it was the same guy panting on the other end, checking to see if you were home so he could come and rape you. Of course, it didn't happen, but while the possibility was there, so was the fear.

But this last call was different. Under the present circumstances, it could have been some monster connected with Talbot and the kidnapping—a truly terrifying thought!

Still, she had expected that if there were going to be a follow-up to the call, it would come quickly. Quite awhile had passed without a sign of anyone below on the street. Besides, the door and windows were locked and there was the gun. It lay ready on the table next to her and all she had to do was clutch it in her hand and fire.

Relax, Relax!

But she couldn't. She had talked to Bryan around five, but why hadn't he phoned again? Well, of course he was caught in the tumult of the search and then there was the ransom arrangement at seven. But that should be long out of the way.

The phone was beside her and she dialled the Columbus. The operator said his line was busy. At least he was there, and that was a small comfort.

Pauline decided that she would feel better if she had something to eat, hungry or not. A sandwich would do. She put down the magazine and stared at the gun. It was an ugly thing, unfamiliar, repulsive. No, she wouldn't take it with her to the kitchen. Too much handling and it might go off accidentally.

There didn't seem to be anything in the refrigerator but some stale cheese. She got down the peanut butter jar and produced bread from the box. She spread, sliced and had taken her first bite of a sandwich when she heard the insistent clang of the door chimes.

Bryan? It couldn't be!

She moved uncertainly into the living room, now plucking the gun from the table and advancing on the door. She stood behind it listening, trying to chew down the sticky remnant of peanut butter sandwich.

Now someone was knocking. It had a most urgent sound. Her palm was moist around the butt of the gun. She couldn't make up her mind if she should answer, so she went to a window and, by opening the blind slightly, was able to peer obliquely out upon the breezeway in front of her door.

The man must have caught the slim ray of light from her window, for he turned his head at that moment. He was very tall and broad of shoulder. His conservative slate-blue suit fitted him with the exactness of good tailoring. He wore a tie and white gloves.

It was not a pretty face, what she could see of it, but then it was not ugly, either. Her reaction to it was one of ambivalence. Certainly the expression was not menacing. But it was authoritative, stern, impatient.

The knocking ceased when the man saw that he was noticed. He simply waited.

She returned to the door and directed the gun toward its centre. "Who is it?" she called.

"Detective Brundage, madam."

A detective! She was totally unprepared for such an announcement. By some crazy chance had the police learned what was going on? Well, it could be a dodge and she wasn't going to fall for it. Bryan said that he and he alone was to be the only one admitted.

She pulled back the spy flap.

"What do you want?" she said.

"Are you Mrs. Pauline Ingram?"

"Miss Pauline Ingram, yes. What is it?"

"It's in reference to a situation I don't wish to discuss through the door, miss."

"Well, I certainly am not going to let you in. I don't believe you're from the police at all."

"I didn't say that I was, miss. You misunderstood. I'm from the William Burns Detective Agency."

She remembered the name—a national agency.

He was taking out his wallet, opening it. "I'd be glad to show you my credentials, Miss Ingram. Mr. Wyckoff sent me—Bryan Wyckoff. He's employed our agency to investigate a matter concerning his father. He thought you might need some—uh—protection, since he's going to be tied up awhile."

"Bryan Wyckoff sent you!"

"That's right, miss."

Well, it simply had to be true! *She* was the only one who knew his real name, including the kidnappers.

"Just a moment, then," she said, and released the flap.

She looked down at the gun in her hand. How silly—was she going to hold a gun on the man while they talked? She crossed the room and shoved it under the newspaper on her desk.

She went back to the door and stood a moment, gulping great breaths of air. Such a relief. Such a relief! Nervously, she out her hair and smoothed her dress.

Then she reached for the bolt to unlock the door.

CHAPTER EIGHTEEN

Bryan swung the Chevy into the driveway of the mansion fronting 326½ Archway Drive. Norma DiNardo's address. He had talked for twenty minutes with his mother and she had said that she absolutely forbade him to call in the police unless his father wasn't released after payment of the ransom. Well, of course he would obey her wishes. But he knew that in some-unforeseen emergency, he would have to use his own judgment.

He pulled up before the garage and cut the lights. He was left in total darkness. It was a pretty grim place after sundown. He could just make out the shadow of the guest house—no lights. Norma DiNardo was still out. Or was she?

He had called her number from the hotel, after speaking with his mother, and the operator had said the line was out of order. That was a new one—it had the smell of trouble. The line had been perfectly okay that morning. There had been no answer, that's all. So he had hurried right out here to investigate. He had meant to ring Pauline but in the excitement he didn't remember until he climbed into her car then didn't want to delay. In any case, he talked with her close to five and she had been all right, nothing unusual to report. She was in a locked apartment, she had a gun and there was a phone handy. He would be with her in twenty minutes.

He got out and didn't understand why he closed the door silently until he realized he was going to break into the place if necessary. It would be a hell of a thing if he got caught. He might have to explain all of it. But then, the whole dismal business was full of risk.

He approached the building on the balls of his feet, wishing now that he had a gun. It was a very gloomy atmosphere, almost too dark for shadows. He reached the door and then just stood there, wondering if it would be ridiculous to knock. He knocked anyway.

In the night stillness the sound was sharp and seemed to carry alarmingly. Reluctantly, he rapped again. The thin door seemed to give under his knuckles. He looked and there was a space between the door and the jamb. He pushed and the door opened.

Well, she had certainly been home since morning. And if she left, she left on the double!

The light switch was no problem. He found it right by the door. Harsh light sprang from an overhead fixture room, maple furniture, much abused. He could see the kitchen, set in an alcove. There could be just one bedroom, the closed door to the left. The layout couldn't bring much over fifty a month.

What next? He didn't quite know. People do occasionally forget to lock doors when they come home, and they do go to bed early if they've been up most of the night before.

He called her name several times just outside the bedroom door. He shrugged and went in. Light from the living room cast a dim radiance upon the bed.

Vaguely he saw her lying there on her back. The queer angle of the head warned him. Still, he was not half expecting the horror which the light revealed when he pressed the switch.

Bryan left the room immediately. He went into the living room and sagged to a chair. For a minute he sat with his head bent, clutching his stomach as if the pressure of his hands would keep him from retching. He thought of nothing. He saw only the grotesque image of the body framed on the closed lids of his eyes.

But when he returned it was not quite as bad. He gave his attention to details—the severed phone cord, undergarments on the floor in a pile, a light seeping from beneath the door of what must be an adjoining bathroom. He entered this and saw that there was blood staining the basin of the sink. Apparently the killer had washed his hands in a hurry.

On the bureau he found a purse containing cosmetics, keys, a letter and nearly five hundred dollars, mostly in large bills. He read the letter: a crude two pages of sex innuendoes. It was signed "Herm." He could not find a return address on the envelope, but there was a scribbled notation of a licence number with the label— "M. J. Talbot."

This was a really important find, the most important since the beginning. So he took the envelope and stuck it in his pocket, returning the letter to the purse.

He couldn't resist the impulse to stare once more at the body—a shuddering mistake.

Then he ran from the room and the house, leaving the door open and the lights blazing.

CHAPTER NINETEEN

Pauline had actually turned the bolt and was reaching to pull the door open when she was struck by a startling thought already on the tip of her mind. Bryan had phoned her just before five o'clock and he had said nothing at all about hiring a private detective!

She flipped the bolt home again and opened the spy

"Sorry to be so long," she said. "But I was changing clothes to go out when you came and I'm not quite dressed. I'll only be a minute."

His face tightened for an instant, then he smiled. "You go right ahead, miss, I'll wait."

"Thank you. Oh, by the way, I haven't heard from Mr. Wyckoff all day and I've been worried. What time did you see him?"

He made a frown of concentration. "Let's see—it was just after two when he came to the office."

"Well, he's upset and terribly busy. He just forgot to call me. Hold on, then. I'll be right with you."

But in the second before she closed the flap, Pauline saw the man's eyes flame in the deep wells from which they peered, the face alerting from bland to predatory, as if a mask had been removed.

He suspects! she thought. *He knows I'm stalling.*

She raced to get the gun from beneath the paper on the desk. But once it was in her hand she felt no relief. If need be, could she shoot this man down like some snarling animal? She didn't know, she didn't know!

The police? There was the phone, right there on the table. Maybe the police could grab this man and put an end to the whole affair. On the other hand, if they merely alarmed him and he got away, what would happen to Bryan's father? Such a scare might ruin all that had gone before.

On tiptoe she moved, gun in hand, to a position behind the

door. Maybe, after all, he would grow nervous and leave. He might. He just might!

Strained by a tension close to hysteria, she inclined her head toward the door, listening. In a moment there was the angry clamour of her door chimes, sounded repeatedly, then silence. A strident knocking followed, then total silence again.

She went softly to a chair and sat on the edge of it, biting her lip until she could taste blood, praying.

Half a minute passed and then her head jerked up. She had heard a thin sound at the window, as if hands explored and tested—another silence. Then muted tapping on the glass, like that of metal wrapped in cloth.

She could no longer think. Her mind was erupting in fear, seething in confusion. She aimed the gun at the sound but her hand shook hopelessly. She placed the weapon in her lap and reached for the phone, dialled Operator.

"Police!" she said. "Emergency—hurry, hurry!"

There was the pulse of the ringing and immediately someone answered. But it was just an operator and she had to be transferred. She yanked her mind from the tapping to concentrate, though now the sound was accompanied by the cracking of glass.

The desk sergeant's voice, when he came on the line, was absurdly calm.

"A man is breaking into my apartment! He—he's going to kill me. I know it. I know it!"

"Name please?"

"Pauline Ingram."

"Address?"

She gave it rapidly.

"What was that street again?"

She repeated.

"Got it! We're on the way!"

"Oh, hurry, hurry!" But the connection was broken.

She heard the glass fall inside the room with a small tinkle and saw it upon the floor beneath the blind, the sound of the window being raised; the clanking of the blind pushed by the man's entering body.

She extended the gun. Amazingly, her hand was now almost steady. The automatic was a type with a visible hammer. She remembered and pulled it back with her thumb.

She saw his legs swing over the sill. Hands lifted the blind and he stood before her.

His eyes flicked to the gun and a spasm of fear twitched a muscle of his cheek. But he had taken what might have been an involuntary step toward her, and she pulled the trigger.

The hammer fell with only a thin snap. She looked at the gun. *What had gone wrong! Didn't Bryan say—?* Then she remembered the slide. She should have pulled it back and released it! For safety, Bryan hadn't wanted to leave the gun with a bullet in the chamber.

She reached to work the mechanism, but it was too late. He bent over her, his hand closed around her wrist and twisted. The gun fell, he picked it up.

"What's the matter, little rabbit?" he said. "Don't you know how to use this? You want me to show you?" He laughed and dropped the gun into his pocket.

"Who are you?" she said numbly. "What do you want?"

"Well," he answered. "We won't have long to get acquainted, but you are a pretty one so you can call me Larry."

Her mind was a

ing to grab one that would give her time. "Larry?" she said.

"That's right, pretty rabbit—Larry."

"Larry Duggan?" It was not really a wild guess. Some instinct had whispered the name.

His face froze. "You know too much, Pauline—far, far too much."

His hand came out of his pocket and a blade sprang at her fece, slim and cunning. She drew back in the chair, gaping in shock. The trembling began again. She felt smothered in a damp blanket of fear.

"Which way is the bedroom, Pauline?"

She was silent. The point of the knife pricked her cheek.

"Which way? Get up and take me there!"

She opened her mouth to plead, but then she looked into his face—and got slowly to her feet. He followed: behind with the knife as she led him down the hall.

"It's here to the right," she said, then hurled herself left into the bathroom, slamming the door, locking it.

"Smart! Smart, Pauline." His voice came sonorously from behind the panel. "But don't worry, sweet, I'll have you out in a jiffy."

She flipped the light switch and searched wildly for a weapon—towels, a cleaning brush, soap—nothing.

She sat down on the edge of the tub and began to weep as his shoulder thundered against the door.

CHAPTER TWENTY

At that moment, Bryan Wyckoff was coming up the steps to Pauline's apartment. He turned at the landing before he reached the door, saw the open window and the shattered glass. He heard the splinter of wood—a door being broken in—a scream. He climbed in. He flew across the living room toward the sound.

The man had Pauline by the hair and was bending her head back. A knife was poised above her throat.

Bryan grabbed him by the collar and clobbered the side of his head so mightily that he fell against the sink, letting go of Pauline. She slid to the floor. The man recovered swiftly and advanced in a crouch, the knife held low.

Bryan didn't like the tight quarters. He backed to the living room. The man followed. Bryan passed the sofa and grabbed a cushion. Holding it as a shield, he stepped in and kicked out. The aim of his kick was beautifully accurate, but the big guy side-stepped gracefully as a dancer and lunged with the knife. Bryan caught the thrust with the cushion and shoved it against the hand. Suddenly he yanked the impaled cushion downward and threw the man off-balance. He moved in close and smashed the side of the man's jaw with a shattering right cross.

The guy stumbled backward, losing the knife. Bryan snatched it up and turned, only to find himself looking into the barrel of his own gun.

"Drop the knife, Buster!"

Bryan obeyed. It clattered to the floor. And on the heels of the sound, a siren wailed, echoed by another.

The man cocked his head, listening. He backed rapidly to the door, reached behind and got it open, vanished. Bryan heard his pounding feet go down the stairs. He ran out to the breezeway in time to see a car catapult from the kerb and rocket into the night.

The two uniformed officers had arrived first, with drawn guns.

But right behind them were two plainclothes detectives of the homicide detail who had been cruising the district and heard the call. The uniformed officers had departed, racing off in the direction taken by the escaping attacker.

Pauline had come out of the bathroom and was sitting weakly on the sofa beside Bryan, her hair tumbled about her face.

'Well, I—I'm awfully glad to see the police," she said to the detectives. "But I'm afraid if my friend here hadn't arrived when he did, you would have been too late. It seemed forever! Why does it take the police so long?"

The tall officer frowned, the stocky officer looked at his watch. "We can't work miracles, lady," he said. "The call came over the radio just about three minutes ago."

"Three minutes!" Pauline looked disbelieving. "Well, that was the longest three minutes of my entire life!"

The stocky officer smiled. "It always seems that way," he agreed, removing a notebook from his pocket. "My name is Sergeant Valletta; this is Detective Legette. Now, you say this man came to your door pretending he was a salesman, and when you wouldn't let him in, he broke in, tried to kill you with this knife."

"Yes."

"And what do you think was his motive? Robbery? Rape?"

"Uh—rape, I suppose. He told me to take him to the bedroom, but I ducked into the bathroom and locked the door. He rammed the door open and that was when he tried to kill me."

"I see." The sergeant examined the knife. "This blade is blood-stained. Were you cut?"

"I don't think so. No, no, I wasn't.

"And you never saw this man before in your life?"

"Never."

"And you, sir. You arrived in the nick of time, as they say. Now, what can you tell us about this business?"

Bryan sighed, glanced apologetically at Pauline.

"I can tell you one hell of a lot," he said. "I don't want to, but I'm going to anyway. Because in the first place, there's been a murder. There might be another and I wouldn't be surprised if you're holding the knife used by the killer."

"Very interesting," said the stocky sergeant, taking a chair. "What's your name?"

"My name is Bryan Wyckoff. My father is Floyd Cameron Wyckoff. And he's been kidnapped ..."

Sergeant Valletta dropped the receiver into the cradle, pushed the phone aside. "We were able to get quite a lot of dope in a hurry, Mr. Wyckoff," he said. "But I can't guarantee it will help."

Bryan and Pauline had gone with him to the station and now were seated before his desk. They had stopped en route to examine the gruesome scene at Norma DiNardo's place. Pauline had remained in the living room, had not looked at the body.

"In the first place," continued Valletta, "the two patrol car boys had no luck catching this Larry Duggan. I didn't really expect they would. Now, we have a line on Duggan. His address in San Francisco for the past few years was a beautiful spot overlooking the bay—San Quentin. A very naughty boy, suspected of almost anything you can name, including murder, but convicted only once for a felony. He had a record of minor arrests, two in Miami. He's a very slick operator—educated, smooth. He jumped parole about three months ago and was believed to be travelling with a couple of petty hoods called "Sailor" Swanson, or Brock Swanson, and Vincent Talapka. Both Talapka and Duggan are former Miamians and know the area well. Nothing at all on Duggan's wife, Bonnie."

"It sounds like we've got everything but the location," said Bryan. "What about the licence number, the one Norma DiNardo wrote down?"

Valletta flipped a page of his notebook. "It's a fifty-nine Dodge sedan, registered to Michael Thomas."

"What address?"

Valletta closed the book. "Not so good. This guy Thomas, Shorty Thomas they call him, has a used car lot on Thirty-sixth Street. The car is from his lot, possibly stolen. I can't say yet. Thomas is being brought in now."

"Fine," said Bryan. "But where does that leave us?"

"Out in no man's land," said Valletta. "Practically nowhere."

CHAPTER TWENTY-ONE

Larry Duggan set the suitcase on the kitchen table, opened it and produced a sheaf of bills.

"Okay, Brock, Vince," he said. "If you guys want to beat it, go ahead. I'll give you two grand apiece and you can take off."

Brock set down his coffee cup with a clatter. "Two grand! Why, that's chicken feed."

"We ought to get at least ten apiece!" cried Vince Talapka. He was a thin, hollow-cheeked man with washed-blue eyes and furrows of skin about his mouth. He had buck teeth and it was the face of a sad, whining bulldog. "You loused up the deal when you scared Ingram into calling the cops. Why should we suffer?"

"Ingram would have signalled the cops anyway," said Bonnie. She poured more coffee from the pot and set a plate of sandwiches on the table. "It stands to reason she knew what was going on. Otherwise, what was she doing with Bryan Wyckoff? She was working with Wyckoff and somehow she got together with DiNardo, too. There's one I'll never figure. But Pauline Ingram was bound to be trouble."

"Two grand apiece," repeated Duggan. "Take it or leave it."

"Suppose we don't wanna take it and we don't wanna leave it," said Brock. He picked up a sandwich, glanced surreptitiously at Bonnie and began to munch.

Duggan dropped the bills and closed the case. He took a stubby .38 revolver from his belt and laid it on top; his hand rested lightly on the butt. He stared at Brock and Talapka in turn.

"Any more questions?" he said. "No? Okay. I just changed my mind. You quit now and you get zero. Stay and you get fifty grand apiece." He fingered the dark bruise on his left jaw. "Listen, you idiots, what's the panic. What could they tell the cops, even if they had the guts? Maybe a fuzzy description of me. You ask half a dozen people what some guy looks like and no two of them agree.

What else have they got? Nothing! No fingerprints, no names, no addresses—dead end."

"Yeah," said Brock. "But once they call 'cop', I figure they'll spill the whole works. Then we've got the newspapers, the FBI, the whole goddamn country on our tails."

"Too hot," said Vince, shaking his head. "Too hot for me."

"All right, hold it, just hold it," said Duggan. "They won't tell the cops anything. They won't dare! And Bonnie's got a new sucker, one of the dames she interviewed and kept on the string just in case. So we send her out tomorrow night We've got a new plan, same kind of gimmick. The girl is dumb, she never can lead to us."

"Maybe not," said Brock. "But just in case, we ought to knock off Wyckoff and dump him in the soup. What can they prove if they don't have a corpse? Hell, why should we gamble now? The thing is set, what's to gain?"

"If they don't deliver," said Duggan, "we can put Wyckoff on the phone again. We can break his arm right over the wire and squeeze the kid for the dough. That's what we gain."

"I think you're wrong, Larry," Bonnie said. "Because if they don't give us the rest of the money now, they never will. They either intend to pay or they don't."

"Yeah," said Vince. "She's right We ought to plug him."

Duggan nodded slowly. "It makes sense," he said. "I like to have a backstop, but it makes sense. I'll think about it. Meantime, we'll discuss the new plan."

CHAPTER TWENTY-TWO

"Now you listen to me, Thomas," said Valletta, shoving a finger under his nose. "In about two minutes I'm gonna pick up this phone and the whole goddamn city is going to fall on you. We've got a murder here and a kidnapping. I can keep your name out or I can wrap it in headlines. And when the newspaper boys finish with you, when they boil you on the front page as an ex-con, what happens to your business? *Wham!* You might just as well blow that lot to hell and gone—good-bye customers, good-bye the nice house and the cushy living. You might just as well leave town!"

Thomas sat hunched in a chair, peering down at his shoes, his bald head glistening in the light. He was a stubby little man, paunchy, with an ancient babyface and sharp black eyes. For half an hour he had evaded with the same story, told over and over again mechanically.

"C'mon, snap to, fella!" said Valletta. "You got one more minute. The Dodge wasn't stolen, you admit that. You just lent it to a customer to drive north with it—to Trenton, you say. And this is such a good customer that you trust him with a Valuable automobile that you could be selling off your lot, and yet you don't even remember his last name—just Gus something. Don't give me that!"

Thomas moistened his lips. "Well, like I said, I don't see the guy but once or twice a year and he's no buddy. Stric'ly business. Besides, it's a crazy foreign name. It'll come to me in a minute. Let me think, sergeant. Just let me think."

"Think about what? A new story? *Hell, no!*" Valletta crossed to the phone, plucked the receiver. "Get me the *Herald,* Jake. As for Charlie—"

"All right, all right," said Thomas.

"Never mind," said Valletta, and hung up. "I'm waiting, Thomas."

"Yeah. Well, I loaned the Dodge to a guy by the name of Vince Talapka. He's got a record and I didn't want no trouble because he—"

"Sure, sure," said Valletta. "You got an address?"

"Of course. You think I'd let him take the heap without leaving his address? I'm not crazy!"

Valletta handed him paper and pencil. "Write it down, write it down!" He grabbed for the phone.

"Jake—find Lieutenant Nagel for me—on the double! Bring Wyckoff and the girl in. And, Jake, you'd better round up the whole goddamn squad. I want every car ready to roll!"

CHAPTER TWENTY-THREE

"Where the hell is Talapka?" said Duggan, coming out of Bonnie's bedroom and closing the door.

"He went down to get some booze," answered Brock. "He knows a bartender who sneaks him a bottle after hours. He should be back any minute."

"We decide to bury Wyckoff and he goes out for booze."

"He's got the shakes," said Brock grinning. "The only dead one he ever saw was his Old Lady and she looked real peaceful."

"He sure *talks* a good game. Tell you what—For kicks, we'll make him do it."

"Why not?" said Brock. "Should be good for a chuckle."

"Vince isn't the only one who gets the shakes when the chips are in the pot," said Duggan. He dipped his head toward the bedroom. "She's practically hiding under the covers."

"Hell, she's only a dame, Dug."

"Listen, she's a lot more dame than you'll ever have, buddy boy."

"Sure. I only meant—"

"Skip it. Let's take a look at Wyckoff."

They entered the room and turned on the light. In the area of face which wasn't covered by a heavy beard, Wyckoff was pallid. His eyes were red-rimmed, dark-circled and puffy. He blinked several times but did not look at them. He gazed at the ceiling and lay motionless in his chains.

"Should we tell him?" said Brock.

"Sure, I'll tell him—We've got news for you Wyckoff. Good news, man. We're gonna set you free. Of course there are all kinds of freedom, Wyckoff. Yours comes in a bullet, calibre .38—in about ten minutes. Wyckoff, six hundred seconds to zero. Start counting!"

Wyckoff turned his head slowly, tried to speak and apparently was unable to. He gestured for Duggan to come close. Duggan leaned over the bed. Wyckoff worked his mouth and spat in his face.

Duggan wiped the spittle calmly. Then he brought the big hammer of his fist up and crashed it down into Wyckoff's face. Blood poured from his nose, but Wyckoff made only a small sound in his throat. Duggan was raising his fist again when Vince Talapka stormed into the room.

"The whole road is alive with cops! Squad cars cruisin' everywhere. I ditched the Caddy in some guy's drive and ran from the back!"

For a long moment Duggan's face was incredulous.

"The rats squealed! But how did they know where to find us?"

He jerked the .38 from his belt. "We've still got the Dodge," he said. "Any chance we could ram on through?"

"Not one in a million." Talapka wiped the sweat from his face. "Cops were piling out a couple hundred yards up the road, comin' this way. They'll be in front by now."

"But the back was clear?"

"Was when I come in."

"Then we'll go that way—on foot!" He snapped the light out and pulled a corner of the shade aside. "Can't see a goddamn thing," he said. "Brock! Kill those lights in the living room! Vince, you get Bonnie in here! Tell 'er to bring that suitcase with the dough."

They bolted through the door and the house became dark. In a moment they were back with Bonnie. She set the suitcase on the floor. In the darkness Duggan lifted the shade.

"What's happened?" said Bonnie. "How could they find us? How could they?"

"Shut up!" Duggan snapped. "There! I saw one. There's another! Okay, let's duck out the back. Brock, you and Vince take the lead, I'll come next, then Bonnie. Stay spread out and shoot anything that moves!"

Shadows in the dark, Brock and Talapka drifted from the room. Duggan picked up the suitcase, moved with Bonnie to the doorway, paused.

He stared for a moment at Wyckoff, who could be seen straining against the chains in the pale wash of light from the window.

Duggan lifted the .38 and took aim.

"No, no!" said Bonnie. "That makes it murder if they catch us."

"I warned them about the cops," said Duggan. "And I like to keep my word." He chuckled. "Besides, if I have to pay, it'll be two for one. I'm worth at least two, eh, Bonnie?"

She grabbed for his arm but he gave her a shove, aimed again and fired.

The sound boomed through the house. Wyckoff jerked and was still.

"Right through the head!" said Duggan. "C'mon, let's go!"

"A shot!" Bryan said. "That sounded like a shot, Lieutenant."

Valletta and Lieutenant Nagle stood with Bryan beside the prowl car. They all gazed toward the darkened house.

"He's right, Lieutenant," said Valletta. "That sure was a shot."

"I'm going up there," said Bryan. "I'm going in!"

"No, you're not, boy," said Nagel. "By this time the house is surrounded. Don't be foolish. They won't get away."

"Stay put, Wyckoff," said Valletta, shifting the riot gun in his hand. "We're ready to close in. Don't be a hero."

"Listen Sergeant," Bryan hissed. "Is that your Old Man up there? Is it?" With a swipe of his hand he grabbed the riot gun from Valletta and began to run toward the house.

He heard Nagels voice. "Hold fire, men!" He loped over the lawn, made the house and bashed a window with the butt of the gun. He reached in and turned the lock, lifted.

At that moment searchlights blazed at the rear of the House. Bryan heard a single shot, followed by two more, then the staccato thumping of a Thompson, the blast of a shotgun, silence.

Bryan launched himself through the window into an empty bedroom. Searchlights were now beamed at the front of the house and he could see clearly. He bounded into the living room.

The figure came toward him from the rear of the house and he raised the gun.

"Don't! Oh, please don't shoot!"

She came into the light and he recognized her instantly. It was Bonnie. He was really tempted to fire, but he lowered the gun.

"You bitch!" he said. "You slimy bitch! Where are the others?"

"Dead," she moaned. "All of them. They're all dead." She

sagged to a chair. "And my father?"

She pointed weakly toward the other bedroom door. He raced to it and sprang into the room.

He saw the blood oozing down from his father's head into the beard and he knew right away, remembered the single shot. He ran back to the living room.

Sobbing, he pulled Bonnie up by the hair, smashing his open hand across her face. He didn't stop until Valletta came up behind and pulled him off. He stumbled back to the bedroom.

Nagel was there, leaning over his father. He was checking his pulse and he lifted an eyelid.

"This man is still alive," he said. "Barely, but he's alive."

"Call an ambulance! For God's sake, call an ambulance!" screamed Bryan.

CHAPTER TWENTY-FOUR

They went up the steps of the hospital together, Pauline moving beside him in silence.

It was early the next evening. Bryan had not been allowed to come until now. There had been an operation the night before. His father had been hovering too close to the edge of death to receive visitors. Even his mother had been advised against flying down for the present. But during the morning his father had been taken off the critical list. He was recovering well enough, but the bullet had entered at a peculiar angle and there was damage to the optic nerve of the left eye.

Bryan turned away from the desk and went to Pauline's chair.

"I won't be long," he said. "They tell me I can only have a minute or two with him."

"I'll wait." She smiled. "Be kind, Bryan. Be kind."

"Of course." He patted her cheek and went down the corridor to an elevator.

"Doctor says you shouldn't tax him, Mr. Wyckoff," the nurse said. "Just a few words, then you must leave."

She smiled pleasantly and opened the door.

The bed had been raised slightly. The top of his father's head and his brow were invisible beneath bandages which also covered the left eye. The right eye seemed to follow his progress across the room with disdain—or did the strangeness of his father's appearance cause him to imagine it?

"Hello, Dad. You look—well, you look a mess." He grinned. "But you're a live mess and that's what matters."

His father didn't answer. The lone eye stared. Bryan brushed the tips of his fingers across the coverlet.

"How does it feel, the *eye?*" Why did he say that? Such a stupid question. "The doctor says you've got a better than fifty-fifty chance to see out of it again."

"Bryan," said his father, "why did you meddle in this?"

Bryan stiffened. "Why? Oh, hell. For kicks."

His father nodded. "I suppose that's it."

"Sure. Same reason you meddled with Bonnie."

He regretted his words instantly when he saw his father's face grow pale, his lips compress as if in pain.

"She was evil, all right," his father said. "But you wouldn't understand how difficult she was to resist."

"Oh, wouldn't I?" Bryan smiled. He suddenly understood a lot of things—about his father, about himself. But how could he explain? How could he tell him he was sorry for all those wasted years of bitterness?

"How's your mother taking all this?"

"She's relieved, of course. I talked to her awhile ago. She'll be here in the morning."

"She doesn't know about Bonnie?"

"No. But I don't see how we can keep it a secret."

"No, we can't," he said wearily. "I've been very unfair to her, Bryan, and she's always stood by me. I can only hope I'll have a chance to make it up to her."

"Yes, Dad, I know," Bryan answered softly. "You didn't ask abut Van. He'll be on the plane with Mother." His father was silent. He looked exhausted.

"Well," Bryan said. "I'll be going now."

His father lifted a pale hand. And when it fell to the bed, Bryan reached and took it in his own, grasping it firmly as if to transfer some of his new-found strength into his father's weakened body and spirit.

"Bryan—I—thank you, son." He pressed Bryan's hand.

Bryan turned and moved toward the door, tears stinging his eyes.

"Bryan?" said his father. "We have to talk. Will you be back tomorrow?"\

"Tomorrow? Sure, if you like."

"Yes ... I'd like that."

Bryan closed the door and leaned against it, struggling to regain control of his emotions. For years he had pushed aside his feelings for his father, and now they came flooding up, overwhelming him.

The nurse came along the hallway toward him. "Oh, thank you

for not talking too long." She said. "I never like to interrupt, but I didn't want you to tire him. He's such a nice man."

"Is he?" said Bryan.

She gave him a quick, appraising look. "Oh, yes. He is—a fine man, and he's very fond of you."

Bryan's eyes widened slightly. "He is?" he asked.

"Yes. He talks about you all the time."

"Oh, you must have me confused with my brother."

"Oh, no. It's Bryan this and Bryan that. He was terribly excited just before you came."

"He was?" Bryan asked, incredulous.

"Yes, indeed. And he said one thing, I'll never forget. Excuse me for being personal, Mr. Wyckoff, but he said: 'Nurse, how do you tell your own son that you love him and that you're sorry, if you've never learned how to say it?' Oh, he's such a very, very nice man!"

Bryan couldn't speak for a moment, and then he said, "Yes, I guess he is—" His voice broke.

Then, to hide his face, he turned and walked down the hall. Pauline was waiting for him. She stood up and looked carefully into his face.

"He's fine, Pauline," he said.

He put his arm around her and they walked quickly down the corridor.

www.ingramcontent.com/pod-product-compliance
Lightning Source LLC
Chambersburg PA
CBHW030635130626
46552CB00002B/869